marriage. The two ...
everything,' he stated bluntly.

'What?' Phoebe stared at him and wondered if she was dreaming.

'I'm suggesting we marry,' he repeated. 'I think it's a good idea.'

For a second, Phoebe's heart hoped. She would belong. With Max and Jake and Josh, here in this house, the four of them together. A family. Oh, wow. Max was asking her to form a family with him. He thought she was worthy of that. He'd seen something in her that made him believe…

Then Max started talking businesslike. 'I'd have pe... sons and you'd be able to... eventually, without worrying about money.'

Is that it? Is that all you think marriage means? Phoebe's excitement sagged and she clamped her lower lip between her teeth, wishing she could clap her hands over her ears and refuse to hear another word. Life never let you off the hook that way, though, so she sat there and tried to look as though he hadn't just offered her the moon and stars, then made her wonder if they were real…

From an early age, Australian author **Jennie Adams** was most at home perched on a gatepost on the family farm with her nose in a book. Her love of reading expanded into writing at age eleven, when she began a four-year tenure as a very bad poet. A gap followed while Jennie pursued a number of careers. Bank officer, piano teacher, and legal secretary to name a few. She met and married the love of her life and had two children, who soon became teenagers who knew everything and who are now the two most treasured young adults in her life. She soon realised she wanted to write the romance novels she loved to read. The pursuit of that dream eventually led to the sale of her first Mills & Boon® novel, THE BOSS'S CONVENIENT BRIDE.

Recent titles by the same author:

THE BOSS'S CONVENIENT BRIDE

PARENTS OF CONVENIENCE

BY
JENNIE ADAMS

MILLS & BOON®

MILLS & BOON and MILLS & BOON with the Rose Device are registered trademarks of the publisher.

*First published in Great Britain 2005
Harlequin Mills & Boon Limited,
Eton House, 18-24 Paradise Road, Richmond, Surrey TW9 1SR*

© Jennifer Ann Ryan 2005

ISBN 0 263 84252 5

*Set in Times Roman 10¼ on 11½ pt.
02-0805-55228*

*Printed and bound in Spain
by Litografia Rosés, S.A., Barcelona*

CHAPTER ONE

'HELLO. One rescue party, delivered to your door and ready to get started.' Phoebe Gilbert examined the two smaller occupants of the room and her heart took a sentimental dive. Max Saunders's sons were gorgeous. She registered that much while one screamed at top volume with his hands clamped over his ears and the other did his utmost to kick the side out of the best recliner chair in the room.

It looked as though Max really needed that helping hand. The man in question had his back turned while he did his best to remove his kicking child from the vicinity of the chair. He didn't hear Phoebe's announcement.

Given the noise level, Phoebe wasn't particularly surprised. She stepped around an upended box of crushed breakfast cereal and a denuded potted plant and moved further into the room.

As she took in the familiar if unusually messy surroundings, a sense of homecoming crashed over her. It was immediately followed by a painful jolt to the solar plexus, because the feeling was false. She had never belonged anywhere in her life, Mountain Gem included. Not that she cared one way or the other.

You're over it, remember? That whole 'wish I had a family' thing is done with.

Phoebe had a creed. *Don't wish for what you can't have.* And who would want to make a family with a woman whose mother hadn't wanted her, whose father hadn't wanted her, and who was barren into the bargain? *Some bargain.*

She gave a defiant shrug. Those days in the orphanage were long since gone. The one decent thing her father had done

5

was to buy her way into boarding school when she'd been eleven.

Nowadays, she had her daycare children. A never-ending stream of little ones to enjoy as she moved from job to job. As long as she didn't get too attached, she survived. Beyond that, she was self-sufficient and proud of it. She didn't need anything more than she already had.

Perhaps coming back to Mountain Gem today had got to her because this visit was so different. In the past, she had felt like the interloper in Max Saunders's home. Not a charity case—she couldn't have stood that—but a visitor. Katherine Saunders's kooky friend. Tolerated by Kath's big brother, but barely. It had been easy to keep her own emotional distance that way, too.

Today, she was here at Max's request. To rescue him. It tipped the scales. Yeah. That must be why these feelings had risen to the surface after she had buried them so well. With a determined sniff she focused her thoughts on the here and now. It was much more interesting, anyway.

'Hello, Max.' She pitched her voice louder. 'I knocked but nobody heard me, so I just came in.'

Even from behind, Max was a commanding presence. Tall. Dark-haired. Broad-shouldered, slim about the hips and with those long, long legs. When he faced her she knew that grey eyes would look directly into hers from beneath winged brows.

Her mouth watered suddenly, and she blinked. *This was Max, for heaven's sake.* The long-time antagonist of her life. The man who drove her crazy every time they met. So what was with the *isn't he gorgeous?* reaction? *That* had never happened to her before!

Enough of this, she decided. She primed her lungs and gave it her best *bellow across five paddocks* effort over the screeching. 'I see the Saunders men are doing their utmost to show the Blue Mountains a good time. Just fancy, two four-year-old boys making more combined racket than an entire Sydney daycare group put together.'

That did the trick. The boys paused momentarily in their noise. And Max whipped around so fast she barely saw the movement. She reacted, though. Her heart paused for a long moment, then restarted at double time.

A sense of panic washed through her and she told herself to wake up. This wasn't attraction. It couldn't be. Her system was just girding up for battle. Yes, that was much more acceptable. 'Hello, Max. I'm here. I'll bet you're pleased I've arrived.'

Max didn't look at all happy to see her, even though he should have been. Instead he stiffened. 'Phoebe.'

The single word, spoken in gravelly accents, managed to convey his deep displeasure at the sight of her.

What was with him, anyway? Didn't he remember this had been his idea? It was not as if she would have dropped everything and cadged a lift out of Sydney to get to him if he hadn't made his need crystal clear. Through Katherine, admittedly, but even so…

She supposed she couldn't expect Max to go too crazy admitting he needed help. It was, after all, the first time he had ever done so, to her knowledge.

And, from her viewpoint, this was about helping the boys, not about Max. When Katherine had phoned Phoebe from America she hadn't only mentioned that Max wasn't coping very well. She had hinted that Max seemed solely focused on getting the boys tidied into some small pocket of his life as quickly as possible.

That worried Phoebe.

Meanwhile, Max was staring at her with that unwelcoming expression still stamped all over him.

'Yes, it's me,' she said. 'In the flesh.' She offered him a view of the point of her chin. 'Given the circumstances, I thought I might have received a warmer welcome.'

She *was* here to turn this chaos around for him, after all. It may have been pure fantasy to believe he would fall down in abject relief at the sight of her, but she had at least expected civility, not an immediate return to their old hostility.

In other words, you got your hopes up and got them whacked back down to size quick smart. Surely you know better than that? Life didn't dish out lollipops, Phoebe had found. You made your own joy, or you did without. She chose to make her own, and usually she did quite well at it.

'You've caught me at a bad moment.' Max ran a hand through dark, already ruffled hair.

Familiar, slightly wavy hair that had always given her itchy fingers, not that it meant anything. She had an appreciation of fine things, that was all. She really couldn't be held accountable for the fact that she found Max aesthetically pleasing. Nor for the fact that her artistic interpretation of Max seemed to be creating more of a problem than usual this visit.

The din was back in full force again. She pitched her voice to rise above it. 'I'd guess you've had a few of those today. Bad moments, that is.' She gestured to a congealed glob of green stuff which was stuck to his shirt and resisted the urge to smirk. Max never got in a mess, in any sense of the word. 'Rough lunch?'

'There was a slight problem with the meal plans, yes.' His eyes narrowed to warning slits and his strong jaw clamped into an uncompromising line.

She had goaded him slightly, she admitted, but just the tiniest bit. In the past he had taken far more from her without letting it get to him. He really *must* be feeling his difficulties.

'If you've come to visit Katherine,' he said, 'I'm afraid you've picked the wrong time. She's not here.'

'Well, yes, I know that.' She pursed her lower lip over her upper. A habit she had when she needed to work out a particular complexity. Why was he pretending that he hadn't expected her?

He waved a hand at the mêlée, which was continuing behind him. 'As you can see, I have my hands full. I don't have time to entertain.'

'What do you mean, entertain?' It was Phoebe's turn to frown. After all, Katherine's request, or rather Max's request made through his sister, had brought Phoebe here. She knew as well as anyone that Katherine was snowbound in Montana and not likely to appear back in Oz any time soon. Yet Max acted as though he hadn't known Phoebe was coming. A sinking feeling started up inside her and quickly took hold.

'Katherine didn't tell you it was me.' It was the only explanation. At the continued incomprehension on Max's face, Phoebe knew she was right. No wonder Katherine had been so cagey on the phone. 'The nanny. Katherine didn't tell you that I was to be the nanny for your boys.'

His face darkened beneath his tan. 'You schemed with Katherine to play nanny to my sons?'

Of all the arrogant nerve! She blinked several times while righteous anger roared through her. 'I answered a plea for help,' she articulated very slowly, as if that would help her to calm down at all. 'Quite a different thing, Max.'

Schemed, indeed! For two pins Phoebe would leave him to his pride, and his problems. Except his boys deserved better than that. They deserved to have proper care, and that field of care just happened to be her speciality.

Any fool could see they were feeling scared and uneasy. Phoebe could fix that and, now that she thought about it, she wasn't going to let the small matter of a short-sighted, incompetent new parent get in her way. Even if that parent *was* Max Saunders. 'It was *your* plea, as it happens.'

'In the first place,' Max growled, 'I don't plead. I certainly never gave out any such plea for help from you.'

She had already figured that out. Phoebe sucked her lungs full of air and got ready to blast him. 'That's not the impression Katherine gave me. She said—'

'Never mind what she said. I can guess.' His face darkened even further. 'I'll kill her.'

'Whatever.' Phoebe wasn't thirteen years old any more. Nor fifteen, nor sixteen, nor even eighteen and, yes, they had fought it out all through those formative years of hers. Had fought over her right to be in charge of herself, even though Max had had nothing to do with the keeping of her. Had fought about politics and economics and dyeing her hair black and orange. And had fought about pretty much everything else as well.

Max was thirteen years her senior. For a while, that had given him an advantage, but eventually she had caught up. Had learned to hold her own ground and started winning her share of the skirmishes.

Now she was a mature twenty-two. An experienced child-care worker and, although he had no idea of it yet, in this case, Max's salvation. She had no intention of allowing him to browbeat her into defeat before she even gave things a try.

Besides, she loved these mountains and this vast sheep and apple farm that had belonged to Saunders family members for generations.

Phoebe refused to acknowledge, even to herself, that she needed to come here sometimes. Just to soak up that oh-so-false feeling of belonging.

Hmph. If *she* owned Mountain Gem she would involve herself hands-on, not leave it to a manager who didn't even live on the same property. It seemed as good a thing as any to get aggressive about right now.

'How's the rare and precious stone business coming?' she sniped. 'Made any more millions lately?' Max had clinched a deal with the elusive Danvers Corporation recently to sell Saunders original jewellery creations through Danvers's Australian stores. Phoebe knew that much because Katherine had told her how pleased Max had been.

Katherine had also mentioned that Max had dated Cameron

Danvers's daughter Felicity once or twice in recent months. Phoebe wondered if Max mixed business and pleasure often, then pushed the thought aside. Why should she be interested in the long line of women who paraded through Max's life, be they past or present?

'I'll set up the video link and have my managerial team give you a report,' Max sniped back over the noise of his boisterous and not at all happy sons. 'Since I've been stuck working from home, that's as close as I ever get to the business. Where would you like to hear from first? Greece? France? Germany?'

He made it sound as though watching over his sons was a real chore. Something he'd had foisted on him and didn't want.

Phoebe paused. Perhaps that was exactly how he felt. If that was the case, it simply underlined how important it was that the boys had someone here who would stand firmly in their corner. 'Actually, Max, I'm not that interested in your business.'

'Trying to goad me, Phoebe?' He offered a smile that was one hundred per cent gleaming irritation. 'If so, you'll have to do better than that.'

'No offence meant.' She gave him the benefit of an unblinking and unrepentant stare. 'I was just expressing my thoughts.'

'Always a dangerous pastime where you're concerned.'

The dart barely made an impact. For one thing, she was used to his barbs. And, for another, he was avoiding the real issue. 'There are other commitments in life that are even more important than making money.'

He glared at her. 'Is there a point to this?'

Phoebe pulled a face. *Not willing to admit a thing, are you, Max?*

'Well, you still look like you need help.' She glanced at the howling and kicking boys. No way would she desert them to Max's ministrations, or lack thereof. 'A lot of it, I'd say. Whatever Katherine may have led us to believe, and I might add she's hoaxed both of us not just you, that fact remains.'

She waved a hand in his direction, determined to take hold of this conversation and steer it the way she wanted.

Enough of this nonsense of him criticising her personality. She already knew she was different—the sort that broke the mould and scared most people off in the process. She didn't need Max to emphasise the point. 'You look as though you haven't slept in days—your hair's all ruffled, you have beard shadow, which is not like you at all, and you're covered in goop.'

Even so, he still managed to look gorgeous. Was it any wonder she needed to let off steam by criticising him? These mixed reactions to Max were enough to drive her crazy. At least *he* wasn't the reason she felt at home here.

Mountain Gem's bush setting, with its gum trees and low scrub, and the sense of stability inside the walls of the old homestead—those were the things that called to her, that could tangle her up, if she didn't watch herself. 'Even *I* didn't get that grotty when I was working with my daycare kids. Whether you want to admit it or not, you need me right now.'

Oh, it felt good to say those words. He would hate having to agree with her.

'What I need,' Max ground out through strong white teeth, 'is a competent, mature nanny. Someone who can help me accustom my sons to life here. They need to settle in, and soon.'

'All nicely compartmentalised? It won't work, you know.' She paused to consider the rest of what he had said. 'And, for your information, I *am* competent. You should see my employer references. I've worked at any number of childcare facilities, and all bar one of them—'

'I admit I've lost three nannies in swift succession.' He interrupted her as though he hadn't even been listening.

Probably he hadn't, since he never took any notice when she tried to prove a point. 'The boys have been ratty. None of the nannies had a lot of experience. Frankly, I don't think you would last any longer with them than the others have.'

'So you'd like me to simply get out of the way?'

Instead of answering straight away, Max glanced down at his shirt, grimaced, tugged it off and wadded it into a ball in one tanned fist. Only then did he meet her gaze, his own unflinching and uncompromising. There wasn't a shred of warmth in it. 'I'm glad you understand. Now that we have that sorted out, I'll see you to the door.'

Suiting action to words he stepped forward, intent, apparently, on manoeuvring her outside with as much haste as possible. The gall of the man left her speechless. So, unfortunately, did the sight of so much of his bare skin.

Phoebe made a concerted effort to pull herself together. 'You're not throwing me out. I won't go.'

She slapped a hand against the centre of his chest, intent on stopping his motion towards the door. Heated, hard male flesh met the pads of her fingers, the palm of her hand.

Big mistake. She drew back, flustered and rather appalled because her body was telling her in a very clear tone that this was a man. One worthy of her feminine interest. On a personal level.

This was no sense of homecoming bothering her now. It was attraction to Max. She may have tried to deny it, but the proof was in her tingling fingers. She was on completely alien territory and had no idea how to cope with the change.

She decided to ignore it, and hope it went away. It had to be some sort of aberration, anyway. So yes, she would just shrug it off and, before she knew it, it would be forgotten. A faded memory, never to be repeated.

'I'm staying, Max, and I'm going to help your sons.' If she focused on the purpose of her presence here she would be just fine. She squared her shoulders and stepped around him.

'I've worked at Sydney Platypus Daycare.' *Until they tossed me out on my ear for having too much of an opinion about everything, but that was the only bad ending I've had in a job so far.* 'Trust me, four-year-old kicking screamers don't frighten me in the least, and nor does their father. You wanted a seasoned childcare worker, and that's what you've got.'

'What I've got is more trouble than I want.' Max muttered the opinion beneath his breath.

Phoebe still heard it and, typically, was goaded into retaliation. 'Don't tell me the famous Maximilian can't balance two small boys and a nanny? Doesn't sound like much of a challenge to me.'

His mouth tightened.

She told herself it served him right. He had asked for it, after all.

Stand aside, Max, and let me show you how things are done.

Besides, she had been having just the slightest bit of trouble finding a new job. When Katherine had told her about Max needing help, Phoebe had been somewhat out of funds, and she had given up her tiny bedsit in Sydney to come here. Not a good time to try to move on elsewhere just now.

Oh, bother Max anyway. This wasn't about him. She deliberately raised her voice without looking at his sons. 'I am *so* hungry. You won't mind if I go to the kitchen and make a big, ugly, sloppy sandwich with heaps of really gooey stuff dripping out the sides and drooling over the floor, will you, Max?'

This question elicited an appalled expression from Max, and startled but definitely interested expressions from both boys. Phoebe breezed past the lot of them to the large kitchen and hauled the fridge door open.

Secretly, she was horrified by the sight of the long, rectangular kitchen. Max prided himself on keeping that room spick and span, but at the moment it rivalled a garbage dump, with mess from floor to ceiling.

She made the best of riffling through the slim pickings inside the fridge, tossing anything edible she could find on to the one bit of service counter that wasn't already cluttered with dirty dishes. All the while she raved about her appetite and how good it would feel to stuff this sandwich down.

'I'll probably even burp loudly at the end, just like a pig,' she added with a fiendish wiggle of her brows.

Max's sons, wide-eyed and encouragingly silent, sidled inside the door, shoulder to shoulder, their gazes locked on the monster sandwich tower Phoebe was assembling with deft hands.

She hoped Max had more supplies stashed in the cupboards than he did in the fridge but, for now, she focused on her sandwich and on getting the two little boys fed so they could give in to their exhaustion and conk out for the night.

Beneath the identical sets of hazel eyes—they must have got those from their late mother—both boys sported dark, weary smudges and overly pale skins. Poor things.

'Mmm hmm. I haven't had a monster sandwich for ten thousand years.' She cut the sandwich into four enormous pieces and crammed as much as she could of the first piece into her mouth, chewing in feigned ecstasy. Actually, it wasn't too bad, given the raw materials. 'All this needs is some milk to wash it down.'

A half bottle of the stuff being the only thing of note now left in the fridge, she helped herself to a plastic mug, which was miraculously still clean and secure in the cupboard, and swilled some down.

'Brilliant. My tummy is starting to feel better already.' She rubbed it appreciatively. 'But then, not just anybody can eat a big monster sandwich like this. Only really brave people can, and people who drink milk as well to wash it down properly in the monster-honoured tradition.'

She glanced at Max and almost laughed at the expression of pure outrage on his face. Didn't he know what she was doing?

Given that he hadn't said anything, she assumed he was so appalled he was speechless. 'Thanks for the food, Max. I'm sure you didn't mind that I helped myself like this.' She grinned at him through her milk moustache.

Inside, she silently warned him not to blow it. The boys were close to capitulating. She could feel it. But if Max went off at her now, goodness knew what would happen.

She wished he would put a shirt on, too, drat it. How could the man be so comfortable in his own skin, and so oblivious to the effect of the sight of that skin on others? Her, for example.

She stuffed more sandwich in before the thought could tumble out of her foolhardy mouth, and rolled her eyes at the boys as she slurped more milk from her mug.

Any moment now they would drop their guards fully and let her start to help them.

And any moment now Phoebe would get past wanting to run her hands all over Max Saunders's bare chest. Sandwiches she could handle. But that other kind of craving was pure trouble.

CHAPTER TWO

'DO YOU suppose we could give some consideration to my sons at some point?' Max glared at the interloper in his kitchen and marvelled that he could want her so badly. His desire to throttle her was as strong as the desire had been earlier to kiss her! The first was perfectly normal. It happened to him all the time. The second was a shock.

This was Phoebe. His sister's untamed and untameable best friend. Normally, the sight of her simply made him want to grind his teeth. He was, in fact, grinding them right now. Well, just look at her, for heaven's sake!

Wild, coarse-looking hair in every shade from blonde to middle brown crowned her head like an unruly mop. In the centre of this display of hairdressing disaster rested an enormous pink bow with a pair of black eyes imprinted on it. When Phoebe moved he got the impression of *two* sets of eyeballs darting this way and that, instead of just one.

She had an elfin face, with a pointy chin that always seemed to be angled to challenge him. Right now, the normally lean cheeks were distended with sandwich and milk coated her upper lip.

'Mmph.' Phoebe chewed, then mumbled something around her sandwich that sounded like, 'We *are* considering your sons.'

'Not in *my* reality, we're not.' Max's gaze moved from her face to her outrageous clothing. Her overalls were such a bright shade of pink they made his eyes ache. The green shirt she wore underneath clashed abominably. And here she was calmly eating him out of house and home while Jake and Josh stood watching, starving. How was that helping the boys?

'Calm down, Max.' Phoebe had finished her mouthful of food and looked ready to take another enormous bite.

She claimed to be here to help. What a joke that was.

'I need round the clock, competent childcare,' Max informed her in a tone that would have made icicles sprout in a scorching desert. 'Not some wraith-like fairy creature with nothing to share but silly monster talk that will probably make my boys cry in the night.'

As if Max needed any more of that. He wasn't cut out for this parent thing. Just look at the mess he had made of trying to raise Katherine after their parents had died. After a few weeks of Max trying to involve himself in her life, his twelve-year-old sister had begged him to go back to working long hours. Jake and Josh's advent into his care hadn't met with any better success.

Max might be great at money but he stank at family. The sooner he got his sons into organised care and returned to his normal way of life, the better it would be for everyone.

First up, he had to get rid of the eating machine, namely Phoebe. Guilt pinched him briefly. Maybe she was eating because she was hungry. She *did* look thinner than the last time he had seen her—what, six months ago? Did she not have enough money?

That thought simply made him angry all over again, for hadn't he tried to ensure her financial security in the past, only to have her toss his efforts back into his face in no uncertain terms?

She was Katherine's friend, Max had plenty of funds and didn't see the problem, but Phoebe was ever Phoebe—stubborn, cantankerous and totally unwilling to listen, even to the most reasonable of ideas.

Like accepting a permanent loan from him to set herself up in a home and get some formal training. Instead she flitted from one poorly paid assistant's job to the next as the mood took her.

'What was Katherine thinking, to encourage you to come here now?'

And why was he still standing here, allowing this farce to go on?

'She was thinking smart. Something you appear to have lost the ability to do at the moment.' Phoebe licked a drop of milk from the corner of her mouth and Max's stomach contracted.

He recognised the feeling. He just didn't understand why it was happening to him. This was *Phoebe*. The bane of his life. He did *not* find her desirable. He simply couldn't.

Liar, liar, his libido chanted.

'I'm not scared of monsters.'

'I'm not, neither.'

Jake and Josh strode towards Phoebe on sturdy small legs, hands fisted on hips, chins stuck out.

'I eat monster s'wiches.'

'I eats 'em too.'

Since they'd arrived a week ago, his sons had alternately played up, cried inconsolably, sulked, and mashed and smashed his house to pieces. Max wondered what form the next outbreak would take, and how many seconds of peace remained until it started.

Phoebe may have got his sons to speak, but her methods were unorthodox and bound to lead to trouble. It would be best if he dispatched her now.

He fixed her with a glare and gestured towards the living room. 'If you're quite finished demolishing my kitchen, we need to talk.'

'Not right now.' She smiled back at him blandly, but with the threat of daggers in her pale blue eyes. Even the spare eyes on her bow seemed to be glaring. 'A person can't simply leave a monster sandwich sitting around the place. It might jump up and run away.'

'Don't make yourself any more ridiculous than you already

are.' Max had had more than enough of her silly talk. Monster sandwiches, indeed.

But the boys giggled at her suggestion. Actually laughed. Their faces crinkled and they chortled for a full few seconds.

Something tugged at Max, deep down in his gut. How was he going to do this? They were so vulnerable, so completely dependent on him. How could he raise them or, rather, find somebody to raise them, who would come somewhere close to making up for his inadequacies? Someone who would allow them to find joy in their lives, to be happy and cheerful and carefree?

'Me eat it,' said Jake.

'Me, too,' Josh added.

'Eat the monster switchwitch.'

'And drink the milk.'

Phoebe hummed and hawed, but offered to share with a gleam in her eye that revealed a certain satisfaction.

Moments later, his sons were eating with every indication of pleasure. They drank a small cup of milk apiece, while Phoebe scooped up dishes and dumped them into the overflowing dishwasher and Max stared, stupefied, his feet rooted to the floor.

Phoebe had only been here minutes and she had the boys literally eating out of her hand. This minor miracle. How had it come about? He had no time to consider further, because as fast as his sons had eaten and drank they drooped, and Phoebe swooped.

'Clean jammies, Max, in the bathroom.' She scooped a boy on to each hip, as though she did it all the time, and swept them away.

By the time Max joined her, bemused, with two pint-sized pairs of pyjamas in his hands, she had washed faces, supervised teeth and stripped two small bodies to the bare minimum. The boys were slipped into their night attire and herded along to their beds.

'I'll be sleeping in the room next door to yours if either of you get scared or decide your beds are too lumpy or anything.' Phoebe gave each child a quick pat and backed towards the door. 'I happen to know my bed is the most comfortable in the house, because I've slept in it heaps of times before.

'See you.' With a wave and a grin she stepped out the door, somehow managing to herd Max with her. As she did so, she brushed against him. Max's body tensed in reaction to her nearness.

'They'll be crying before you can say boo.' He stood in the corridor, waiting for the yells of rage or screeches of fear, but they didn't come.

That just left Max, trying to deal with wanting Phoebe and wanting her out of his house in roughly equal measures. Or he told himself the balance was about fifty-fifty.

'I'm too tired to deal with you tonight.' He grumbled the words at her gracelessly, a counterpart to his body's unwelcome reaction to her. She was his sister's best friend, not to mention all wrong for Max in every way it was possible to imagine.

He did not need to desire her on top of every other thing going on in his life at present. 'Now that they're asleep I can't leave them in order to drive you back into town, either. Brent—my new gardener—was going out for the evening, so I can't ask him to do it. You'll have to go tomorrow.'

'No need to thank me. *Yet*.' Phoebe stepped past him into the doorway of the room she always used when she visited, which, thank God, Max thought, hadn't been often lately.

'I realise your pride must be tangled around your ankles right now,' she added. 'Get some sleep. Maybe tomorrow you'll be able to accept that I'm the best thing that's happened to you this week.'

'You're not staying.' The forceful words were a wasted effort because she'd closed the door in his face.

Disgusted, speechless, Max stared at it. Who did she think she was, anyway?

It was more of a splintering sound than an all-out crunch. In fact, as accidents went, this one almost registered as a non-event. Until Phoebe looked over her shoulder and saw the damage.

'Oh, poop. I'm in trouble now.' She had her hand on the door latch of Max's monster four-wheel drive, preparing to get out, before she remembered what she had, for a split second, forgotten. She wasn't alone.

Her two small charges didn't hesitate to offer their reminders, gleefully, from the back seat of the Range Rover.

'Poop, poop, poop,' Josh crowed, getting louder with each use of the word. 'Poop, poop, *poop*!'

'You crunched it.' This came from Jake, who had managed to slither himself around enough in his car seat to survey the farmhouse's wrecked veranda latticing. 'Max be mad. Mad, mad, *mad*.'

Phoebe grimaced a smile into the rearview mirror at the identical mirthful faces. *Isn't it great that they feel safe and happy enough to express themselves to me this morning?*

'It's probably best if you don't say poop too often, Josh,' she corrected automatically. 'Words like that are really best left for the big people. And, Jake, Max is your father, as I've already explained several times today. You address him as Dad or Daddy, not Max, and you don't know if he'll be mad because he hasn't seen the damage yet.'

Phoebe knew, but that wasn't the point. She had been doing so well today, too. She had got the boys up, had dressed them and herded them outside, all the while allowing Max to sleep. Total consideration, that was what she had delivered to him.

She had then forced herself to drive his enormous car to the nearest reasonably sized town, despite her trepidation at getting behind the wheel of something so intimidatingly large.

With almost the last of her own dwindling funds, she had bought the boys' breakfast and stocked up on a few necessities. All of this to help out, but would Max think about that now? She doubted it.

Phoebe didn't want to admit that she might have wanted, even slightly, to gain Max's approval for her extra efforts. What would be the point of that?

She kicked the toe of one booted foot against the brake pedal in frustration. 'It's his fault anyway, for letting the foodstuffs run out that way. No cereal in the cupboards. Barely any milk, no bread, no fruit. What was he thinking?'

She refused to acknowledge any other feelings. Like dread, anxiety or guilt. Those were for the past, for an uneasy teenager who hadn't felt at home with herself, let alone with anyone else, and especially not here, under Max's ever watchful eye.

'Katherine's friendship was worth it,' she muttered. Meanwhile, there was only one thing for it, she decided. She had to get to Max before he got to her.

'Jake, Josh.' She fixed the boys with her most practised stern expression. 'Wait here until I'm ready to get you out. Do not move. Understand?'

Phoebe emerged from the vehicle into the cool morning air and drew a deep, calming breath. A young man was working inside one of the sheds in the distance, but didn't appear to have noticed her. Brent—the new gardener? At least he hadn't witnessed the result of her rush of overconfidence.

What had she been thinking about, to try to back the vehicle up to the steps that way? She couldn't even see over the headrest. 'Oh, well. Might as well go face the music.'

As she started towards the house Max came charging out. An ominous-looking frown marred his face. Jeans, sturdy boots and a dark T-shirt all appeared to have been pulled on in a hurry, and his hair stood on end. Straight from his bed,

Phoebe decided, and told her raging hormones to get over it. Like, for ever!

'Why am I not surprised to see my car butted up to the veranda, which is now completely smashed to bits?' Max's question cut through the space separating them. 'Oh, that's right,' he added. 'It's because *you're* in residence.'

His gaze moved to his sons, who were still peering, grinning, over the backs of their booster seats. 'I knew you'd be a bad influence and here's the proof, not even twenty-four hours later. I don't suppose you'd care to explain what you were thinking.'

'I knew you'd react like this. How predictable.' She may have been slightly in the wrong in this particular skirmish but, even so, Phoebe wasn't about to admit it.

They met nose to nose at the foot of the veranda.

'What's predictable is you taking my car and mangling things with it.' Max pointed to the four-wheel drive, then at the latticework, which was lying in fragments on the ground. 'Look what you've done. You know you're not a good driver. You should never have got into it.'

'If I'm a bad driver, and I'm not saying that I am because I'm not, you can thank yourself for it.' Did he think having this happen had made *her* happy, either? It had been a well-intentioned accident. Couldn't Max at least try to see that? 'You're the one who attempted to teach me and proved you weren't man enough to do a good job. And I took the car to help you, as it happens.'

'I don't see how crashing my car could possibly be helping me,' Max said sarcastically. 'And, for your information, I faced my mortality on a regular basis for months at a time for your sake so you could learn to drive. These are the thanks I get, apparently.'

Oh, good. Heap the guilt on, why don't you? She screwed her face up into an aggressive moue. 'I was stocking up on groceries.'

'Is that my fault? You ate the entire kitchen for your dinner last night.'

'I did not.' She stamped her foot.

Max's gaze roved over her, from the blue jeans down to the hiking boots and rust-coloured socks, then back up and over the bright orange tie-dyed cheesecloth shirt.

His anger seemed to reach fresh heights. 'You're naked underneath those clothes.'

'And you're irrational, as ever.' She paused and blinked. In fact, it *had* been a very strange thing for him to say.

Suddenly all yesterday's heated reaction was back in force. Drat Max for reminding her. Phoebe tried not to think about nakedness and Max, but didn't do very well. She took a shaky breath.

'If I'm irrational,' Max said slowly and clearly, 'it's because you make a nutcase out of me any time we're within shouting range of each other.'

Okay, well, maybe that brought things back into perspective a bit. If she could just settle her ruffled pheromones back into place, everything should be fine. Sort of.

'In range,' she repeated. 'Um, yes.'

They were certainly in range now. So close together that she could see right into his eyes, could see the storminess and the sudden darkening as he stared down at her. Her breath caught, and she tried to whip her indignation back around her. *I do not want to kiss him!*

'I'll pay for the damage to your car and the veranda, Max.' She stepped away from him and waved a hand as though she dealt with this kind of thing every day. And as though she wasn't in the least disturbed by his nearness.

'Don't bother about the cost. I'll fix it myself.' Max's hands came up to rest on his slim hips. 'How did you get here yesterday, by the way?'

What did he care? She shrugged. 'I hitched, of course.'

'That's dangerous.' Disapproval radiated from him.

'Hitching's not dangerous when you know the driver well enough to trust him or her.' She glared right back. 'And don't try to distract me. I'll pay for the damage to the car and the veranda. I take responsibility for my actions, unlike some people I could name.'

'Like newly appointed parents, you mean?' His tone warned her to back off, fast.

Instead, she nodded and swept him with what she hoped was a shrivelling look. 'Yes, exactly like that. I wonder what your latest female friend thinks of the two new acquisitions to your home?'

'There is no...' He trailed off, shook his head, and pushed out one arm in a wide, dismissive arc. 'You're criticising me. Again. Don't you ever get tired of it?'

'It's justified.' Phoebe poked him in the chest with one finger. This had been coming since she arrived last night. Since before then, actually, when Katherine had first told her that Max had suddenly discovered he was a father. She might as well get it out in the open and be done with it. 'It's not like you've exactly proved to be the commitment type in the past, is it? One girlfriend after the next, and none of them lasting beyond their first hint that they'd like something more from you than sex and a rapid farewell. It's no wonder you weren't told you were a father, even if I *am* surprised that you were careless about something like that.' She prodded him with her finger again. 'Do you even *want* them, Max? You certainly don't act like it.'

As the words tumbled out, she realised she had gone too far and wished she could take them back. Max's face slowly blanked of all expression, until only a stark, hard-edged mask remained.

'I think it's time I put a stop to this,' he said in a voice that was chilling in its calmness. His hand snaked out and wrapped around her arm. 'Before I lose my temper. As for my sex life, it's no business of yours.'

'Am I supposed to be scared?' She fell back on bravado and hoped it would work.

Max simply glared at her. 'That might be a good idea.'

'Well, I'm not scared. Far from it.' She tugged at her arm and he let it go.

Phoebe couldn't let the conversation go, though. She ploughed on, well aware that she was in dangerous territory, but she needed to know this. 'Do you deny that you're just trying to push your sons off on to a nanny so you can ignore them? You can't just bury yourself in work, in your old way of life, and pretend everything else doesn't exist.'

For a moment he didn't speak. When he did, his words were cold, his eyes hard and unyielding. 'I will make the choices for my sons that I believe are in their best interests and that, Phoebe, is not something I will justify to you or negotiate about.'

Although he still looked angry, Phoebe also got the impression she had hurt him. Regret unfurled inside her. 'Max.' She stretched out a hand.

He ignored it and stepped back, gesturing towards the back of the car. 'My sons are getting restless. Maybe you should get them out of the car, if you're quite finished with this little *discussion*.'

'What about you?' She bit her lip. 'What are you going to do now?'

'I'm going inside to phone around for a new nanny. What else?'

The dart found its mark, although she tried hard not to show it. She didn't want to go. Stupid, wasn't it, to want to hang around here? All that was likely to happen if she did was that she would get too attached to Max's sons and be upset when she had to leave them.

Phoebe tried, but sometimes her overactive mothering instinct didn't exactly stay under control as well as she wanted it to. Empty womb syndrome, she thought, trying to be cynical and failing utterly.

She refused to admit that she might not want to leave Max either.

'Whatever you feel is best, Max.' She lifted one shoulder and let it drop. 'The only thing I care about is that your boys are in the best hands.' A hint of steel crept into her voice. 'And *that* is something that I will make absolutely sure of, no matter what.'

He shook his head. 'Do I really need to remind you that you don't even have a say in this?'

Indeed, she didn't have a say. They weren't her sons. She had no hold on them whatsoever, despite the fact that they had crept into a corner of her heart already, just by being their cute, irascible selves.

Phoebe had no business feeling attached to Max, either, even if it was only physical attraction. And it *was* only that, she assured herself. Which was bad enough.

'You can say what you want.' She returned him stare for stare, determined that he wouldn't guess he had hit a raw patch with that last question. 'It won't change my attitude one iota.'

'Won't it? We'll see about that.' Max turned on his heel and walked away.

CHAPTER THREE

'FINE. Let Max get his new nanny and bring her back here and send me packing. As if I care about it.' Phoebe tossed the damp towel in the hamper, hitched her old nightshirt back on to her shoulder where it had slipped down, and stepped out of the bathroom into the hallway.

Max had been gone all day. He had stalked to his study after their altercation, then left a while later, without so much as a by your leave and looking grim enough that she had decided to keep out of his way.

He hadn't returned since and, even as Phoebe thought about this, irritation flared afresh.

She paused to peek into the boys' room and nodded with satisfaction when she saw that both Jake and Josh were still soundly asleep. That little tug thing happened in her heart again, and she sighed. The boys had been a gift to her for such a short time.

'I'll get over it.' But she didn't feel particularly reconciled. In fact, the more she thought about this whole day, and the previous evening, too, the angrier she became all over again.

'The man doesn't want me here,' she muttered, stalking determinedly away from the bedroom with the two sleeping forms in it. 'He doesn't trust me to do a good job, yet he leaves me alone with his sons all day and doesn't even tell me where he's going. As if I *wouldn't* start to fall for them when he leaves the field clear for me like that.'

It was Max's fault that she was struggling not to care. All his! Phoebe hurried on towards the kitchen and the promise of a cup of soothing tea before she turned in to bed. Today would doubtless be her last in the role of nanny here. After that, all these inner turmoils would be a moot point, anyway.

A light shone at the end of the kitchen. Max sat at the table, eating the meal she had set aside for him and poring over a batch of documents. He must have got back while she'd been showering.

'Where's the new nanny? I thought you'd have brought her with you.' Phoebe paused in the doorway, her bare feet braced on the vinyl flooring. The room was cool, the large windows over the sink reflecting the inky blackness outside.

Max wasn't quite as cool. His expression reflected both weariness and heat. The latter set her senses on alert, and she pulled an irritated face at herself. *Not now, okay?* As if she didn't have enough on her mind.

She couldn't help thinking that Max was affected too, though, which only made it tougher for her to distance herself from her reactions to him. It amazed her that Max could want her, even on the most basic of levels. Things had changed. She didn't quite know why, but something told her there would never be any going back to the way they used to be.

What did that leave, though? She certainly wasn't interested in becoming one of his many fly-by-night involvements. Fortunately, she could control these random reactions to him. Provided she kept her distance, she was under no threat.

'Thanks for leaving me a meal.' Max glanced back down at his plate, then up again. 'I didn't expect you to go to any trouble.'

'Believe it or not, I can be quite organised when I try.' Phoebe relaxed somewhat, confident in her ability to hold her foolish reactions to him at bay. 'I didn't actually find it too dramatic to cook enough food for four dinners instead of three, even with such limited resources to choose from.'

It seemed best to try not to dwell on the fact that her skin was tingling simply because Max was near.

She came further into the room, noticing for the first time

the clutter of bulging shopping bags at the far end. Max had apparently, at some point during his day-long absence, found time to stock up on grocery supplies. 'You haven't answered my question. Do you have a new nanny organised?'

He pushed his plate and the documents aside and gestured for her to join him.

She did. Reluctantly. Nobody liked to be fired, after all, and that was what Max was bound to do to her any moment now.

Up close, Max looked even more tired, and she acknowledged that her presence here hadn't helped him, much as she had believed it could. Even though she still believed she could assist him a great deal with his sons, it wasn't going to happen.

Phoebe decided that she would rather bow out of her own accord than have Max push her. Given their propensity towards wanting to kill each other on sight, she supposed it was no surprise that Max didn't want her here.

The inexplicable heat they seemed to be generating between them was simply another complication to pile on to the rest. Max didn't like complications. Phoebe didn't either, really.

Still, something in the region of her heart ached at the thought of leaving. She told herself to ignore it. Just so long as Max had made acceptable arrangements. The boys had to come first, no matter what.

'I can be out of here any time you want, Max.' There. She had made it easy for him, and it barely felt like cutting out a piece of herself at all. Phoebe was used to taking care of herself. This time would be no different. 'I only came to help you because I thought you wanted me and were in a bad way.'

'I *was* in a bad way.' The admission was gruff.

'Yes, you were in a mess.' She smiled to let him know she meant no malice by the comment. 'For what it's worth, Jake and Josh have had a reasonable day. I did my best to keep them busy.'

'And cleaned up most of the house while you were at it.' He shook his head. 'You didn't have to—'

'I know.' Even so, it had been kind of fun, playing house for a while in something larger than a shoe box. Dangerous, too, though, because playing house was too close to playing happy families. To falling in love with the boys. To wanting Max, and aching for things she could never have.

Argh! Phoebe suppressed the aggravated screech building up inside her. She must need to get out in the sunshine more or something. Build up the happy vibes inside her head and put a stop to these underrated, overdramatised, ridiculous yearnings.

'Sometimes it's better for little children to get the feeling that you're simply going about your business,' she said, pulling herself back to the conversation with some difficulty, 'with them tagging along. It takes the pressure off them a bit. Anyway, it was just for the day.'

Now that the time had come to bow out she found it difficult to come up with the right words, but she promised herself she would get there somehow. No way would she allow Max to even suspect that she didn't want to move on. 'So, when does the new nanny arrive? Tonight? Is she from Sydney? Travelling out by car? I can be out of your hair in no time.' *Once I check her over and decide she's okay.* 'You'll barely notice I've been here.'

This seemed to amuse Max, for he glanced at her in a rather comprehensive way and shook his head. 'You're a lot of things, Phoebe, but unnoticeable isn't one of them. Everything about you draws attention, whether you intend it to or not.'

'I don't see how that can be true.' Or at least not in a positive way. Basically, she considered herself to be a mere blob on the greater canvas of life. If she were to be abducted by aliens tomorrow, who would even care? Katherine, she supposed, but that was about it. Max would probably send the aliens a sympathy card.

Max's rich laugh rang out. 'Don't you? What about the way you dress, for starters?'

'Dress?' Oh, that. She chose her clothing from second-hand shops mostly, or bought cheap from warehouses when she got the chance. 'I admit I don't dress like a business executive, but then—' she shrugged '—I'm not one.'

'The guitar and the emblem? Those are not attention-getters?'

For a moment she didn't understand what he was talking about. She certainly wasn't any kind of musician. Then she glanced down at her T-shirt. Although faded now, it sported a screen print of an electric guitar, with the words *Bite Me* emblazoned across the front.

'This thing?' She shrugged. 'It was, um, a gift from a band member I knew once. I could hardly refuse to wear it.'

With Max examining the article so thoroughly, she felt very aware of her bareness underneath.

To distract herself, she peered across the kitchen at the groceries and noticed a bag overflowing with bananas. 'Are you sure you haven't overdone it on the fruit? I hope half of that doesn't go to waste.'

Max followed the direction of her gaze. 'I bought them for the banana-smoothie freak.'

'What? But I won't be here.' Banana smoothies were a long-time passion of hers, a fact that both Max and Katherine knew well. Phoebe stood up and padded across the room to poke the bag with one foot.

Did he mean to give her the bananas as some sort of parting gift? Then a different thought occurred. 'Oh. Does the new nanny like banana smoothies too?'

'There is no new nanny.' Max joined her beside the pile of bags. His voice roughened to a gruff rumble. 'There's just you and a heap of bananas. You might as well stay long enough to eat them.'

It wasn't the warmest invitation-cum-job-affirmation she had ever had. And it was painfully temporary. Despite all this, her heart lifted. She could stay. Help the boys. Enjoy....

Hello. Stop sign, here. No dreaming the impossible, remember?

'What happened? Did the boys' reputations scare off all the contenders?' She didn't mean that. In fact, she felt Max had greatly exaggerated any behavioural challenges they may have displayed since they'd arrived.

Frankly, they struck her as two very normal, very vigorous little boys who'd recently lost their mother and didn't quite know what to do with their new surroundings. 'No, even though they're a little out of sorts at the moment, I find that hard to believe. You must be looking in the wrong places.'

'Trust me, I looked. I asked. I phoned around.'

'For an hour tops this morning, then you disappeared. Are you telling me you spent all day scouring agencies and came home empty-handed?' Foolishly, a part of her needed to believe that Max had really wanted to keep *her* on. She slapped that part down hard.

'I started. I met a few people.' Frustration filtered into Max's tone. 'An old bag with a pursed-up mouth, a woman who was so out of shape she got puffed getting out of her chair. Cranky nannies, stupid ones, disciplinarians in sheep's clothing.'

He made a chopping motion with his hand. 'It wasn't working. None of them felt right. I gave up and spent the afternoon at my office, trying to get some work done and figure out what to do about this problem. Neither of which effort was particularly successful.'

'I see.' And Phoebe thought she probably did. In the face of all those problematical nannies and his unsatisfactory time at work, Max had stockpiled on bananas and come back to regroup. To get his plan honed down to razor sharpness before he went out and snaffled not just a good nanny but a nanny *par excellence*, tailored to his exact requirements.

That made a rather Max kind of sense. 'You need time to sort things out? You'd like me to hang around until you can do that? A few days, maybe.' For good or bad, she didn't even hesitate. 'I'll do it.'

For the boys, she added silently, *but only in the same way any responsible childcare worker would care about them.* It was a belated effort to justify her decision. She was about to say more when a shaft of moonlight outside the window drew her attention to a number of bulky boxes. 'What's all that?'

Max followed the direction of her gaze. 'It's a climbing frame for the boys. It has to be assembled, but I should be able to knock that out in a couple of hours tomorrow.'

Wow. She hadn't expected him to think of something like that. 'Good idea. It'll give them something to expend their energy on other than kicking in your furniture and screaming the house down.'

He grimaced. 'That was the idea, and I have to have something to keep me occupied while I work out what to do with them.'

Some force compelled her to tell him, 'You could be a brilliant father, Max, if you just let yourself—'

'Don't.' He trapped her in an angry gaze. 'Don't tell me what I can and can't do, or be.'

Well, she supposed she had asked for that. Acknowledging his answer didn't make it any more palatable, though. *Why couldn't he just love them, accept them? Instead of trying so hard to keep them at arms' length?*

Was she asking about his boys now, or about herself? The boys, of course! Phoebe had sorted out her own life history long ago and, she might add, none of it had anything to do with Max. Drat it, whatever bee had got in her brain box, she wished it would get back out again.

'I'll help you as much as I can.' That was what mattered most right now. When he turned to face her, she offered a small smile. 'It's what I came here for.'

She laughed a little, just to show she didn't care too much. That she wasn't still just a little bit worried that getting to play families any longer might cause problems for her later. 'Until you get a new nanny, that is.'

'Thank you, Phoebe. I appreciate your willingness to try.' The words may almost have choked him—she didn't know— but at least he gave it a go. 'And it would be a shame to waste the bananas.'

If Max could attempt a joke, the least she could do was be gracious. In the spirit of the moment, she stuck out her hand. 'To my tenure as temporary nanny, then.'

Max took her hand in his. 'To getting my sons settled.'

Their opinions on the term *settled* didn't exactly line up, but Phoebe nodded anyway, then retrieved her hand from the disturbing contact with his. 'May I ask you some questions?'

Now might not be the best time, but when would be better? Max was in a reasonably mellow frame of mind, they were trying to get along and the boys weren't here to eavesdrop on the conversation.

'What is it that you want to know?'

'I'd like you to tell me about their mother.' *Did you love her? Was she in love with you? Are you still in love with her? Or was she just like all the others? Can you not even remember what she looked like properly?*

Phoebe told herself she wanted to know for the boys' sakes, but it wasn't entirely true. She wanted to know how Max had felt about the woman who had mothered his children. And she wanted to know what kind of woman had given birth to Max's sons. Had nursed them through the baby illnesses and toddling scrapes and bruises.

What Phoebe wouldn't give for a chance at all of that. After all her careful thoughts, Phoebe was disgusted to realise she was jealous of someone who wasn't even alive any more. Of someone who had been close to Max once in a way Phoebe would never be.

Are you mad?

She had to be, to even consider wanting that kind of relationship with him. Max didn't stay with women, she warned herself. Phoebe shouldn't have asked about the boys' mother. Shouldn't have opened up the subject. Except that the boys needed to be able to deal with their feelings. So she explained, 'If I'm to help Jake and Josh to adjust to the changes taking place in their lives, I need to understand a bit about their mother.'

'Maryellen was a university lecturer who happened to have an interest in precious gems, particularly in some of the more unique settings such as Saunders Enterprises provides.' A muscle in Max's jaw tightened. She got the feeling he didn't really want to be talking about this but, even so, he held her gaze. 'I met her at a special display evening of some of our more unique Australian opal designs.'

His comments revealed nothing of what he may have felt towards Maryellen. Was that because he hadn't cared about her really?

'I suppose she was gorgeous.' The words bubbled out before Phoebe could stop them.

Max's shrug confirmed it. 'We had a brief affair. She was a career woman to the core. She certainly wasn't interested in commitment and neither was I. At the end of her visit to Sydney, we parted amicably and I forgot about her until the day her lawyers contacted me, informing me of her death, my paternity and the expectation that I should collect my sons immediately.'

So Maryellen *had* just been another in the long line of Max's conquests, but perhaps, if Max had known she was having his children, that might have been different. Oh,

Phoebe just wished she could stop worrying at the whole issue!

Max blew out a long breath. 'The boys were in the care of the nanny Maryellen had used but she was a teenager, relying on her mother to help her until I got there. It was far from an ideal situation.'

Tension radiated from Max's big body and he clamped his jaw down hard. 'Discovering I was a father came as a shock, but it shocked me more that Maryellen never contacted me. I thought she knew me well enough...'

Apparently Max had thought they'd had some kind of connection. 'Does this mean you're secure in terms of custody?' Phoebe wanted to know.

'Yes. Maryellen had no other family and I was named as sole guardian and also noted on their birth certificates as their father. There's no doubt that they're my responsibility.'

What a sad way to put it. What an even sadder thing it was that if Maryellen hadn't died Max might very likely never have known he had sons. 'I'm sorry, Max.'

'It doesn't matter.' His expression became fierce for a moment before he smoothed it back into bland indifference. 'All that counts now is that I do my best for them.'

How did he reconcile that with wanting to dump them off on to a nanny? 'Just one other thing. I'm sorry to ask, but how did Maryellen die?'

'An accident at an archaeological site. The boys weren't with her at the time.'

Phoebe didn't want to think about it any more. Her emotions had jumped back and forth quite enough for one day. 'I'll say goodnight, Max. It's getting late and I'm sure the boys will be up with the kookaburras in the morning.'

'Thank you, Phoebe.' Max caught her arm as she moved to pass him, staying her. 'For agreeing to remain here for now.'

A lot went unsaid in those few words. Their antagonism

and attraction. The fact that it wouldn't be easy. That they were both on uncharted ground in this.

'You're welcome.' She looked up at him, thinking that would be the end of it. But something in his gaze changed and he bent his head, probably to drop a kiss on her cheek.

Okay. It would be a novel experience, Max being nice, but she would do her best not to keel over with shock. Phoebe braced to receive the salute, then felt her breath hitch as his lips met not her cheek, but her mouth. The feelings that bombarded her then, stunned her to her toes.

All she could think, was, *Oh, my goodness, oh, my goodness, oh-my-goodness!* She was going into shock, or cardiac arrest or something. Her breath stuttered, a shiver started at the base of her neck and quickly suffused her.

Max's hands gripped her shoulders, holding her still while his mouth moulded to hers in slow, steady exploration. No wonder women got involved with him, even though he was a love 'em and leave 'em type. The man's kisses were dynamite.

Phoebe melted into him, into the kiss. Like a big old blob of butter in a pan. Why, oh why, had he done it? Why did he continue it, even now as her bones melted?

It was Max, not Mountain Gem or Katherine or any of the rest of it, that gave her that feeling of coming home. The thought came from nowhere. She denied it instantly. It couldn't be that. This was a potent kiss, from an experienced man, that was all.

And oh, boy, it really was all that. She lost her concentration in the heat of it. Sensations bombarded her from all sides. The touch of those warm, firm lips, pressed so intimately against her own. The scrape of his jaw against her softer skin.

His fingers moved to her chin, angling it as he kissed her, and she wanted to be angled and kissed more and still more.

For a moment insanity took her, and she kissed him back with all her worth. Their bodies pressed together and his arms crushed her close. Heat roared through her, burning her up until she was almost convinced she could smell scorched butter. But sense and reason came back eventually, and with them an all-important question. Two, actually.

What was she doing?

And with Max, of all people?

'No.' She wrenched away on a gasp, horrified by her own complicity and thoroughly uneasy with Max's behaviour. Was he lost in thoughts of Maryellen? Had that made him kiss Phoebe? A sort of misplaced guilt or resentment or something?

All Phoebe knew was that she had almost become crazy for a moment there. Had almost believed that there was something about Max that she had to have to survive. Madness. Sheer idiotic lunacy. It was just as well she had come back to her senses before things went any further.

Max appeared as stunned as her, his face etched in taut lines as he stared at her, breathing hard. 'That was—' He broke off, raked both hands through his hair as though all the demons of hell had come to roost on him at once.

Then he forcibly rearranged his facial muscles. Rolled his shoulders. Sucked in a deep breath and blew it out again. 'So you'll be helping out as the nanny until I can get a replacement. I'll payroll you at the same rate I offered the others.'

He named a figure.

Phoebe nodded without taking it in. Back to business was good, if only she could get even a single part of her to change to the appropriate channel, instead of getting stuck on FM One-Oh-Kiss!

'Good.' Max inclined his head and took a step backwards, then another. 'Great. That's settled then. That's all…settled.'

'Settled,' Phoebe parroted and, for good measure, nodded just as Max had done. She was still in shock, her senses reeling, some unhelpful part of her suggesting that Max's kiss was something she might like to repeat. Right now, even. 'It's business, right?'

'Yes.' Max pushed his hands into his pockets and studied the painting on the wall to her left. 'That's right.' His gaze tracked over her and, once she was thoroughly singed, moved away again. 'It's business.'

Good. They could forget this had ever happened. That was best. Because clearly Phoebe couldn't afford to be attracted to Max. Not when it resulted in this kind of impact on her.

She would keep right out of his path in future, metaphorically speaking. Keep it businesslike. Avoid all thoughts of intimacy. And, while she was at it, she would avoid all comparisons between Max, his sons and herself and any kind of happy families.

Max wanted to payroll a nanny. For now, Phoebe was that person. She would think of the job as clocking in, clocking out. A business arrangement, no feelings involved. She could do that. Right? 'That's all organised, then.' She tried for some sort of distant nonchalance, failed utterly and decided to cut and run instead. 'Uh, I'll see you around,' she said, and fled.

CHAPTER FOUR

AS GOOD as his word, Max erected the play equipment bright and early the next morning. By the time Phoebe got the boys through breakfast and a minor case of the whinges and moved to the window to look out, the job was done. Max was standing back, examining his handiwork with a thoughtful expression on his face.

At least his attention wasn't centred on her, Phoebe couldn't help thinking. After yesterday's kiss, and what had followed, Phoebe was determined not to melt again. She had given herself a good talking to and hoped it wouldn't happen, but if she did start to turn mushy around the edges she would prefer the chance to get herself under control again without Max noticing her dilemma.

She was determined to keep some sort of emotional distance from the boys, too. Phoebe finished the last of her banana smoothie and wondered how long it would take Josh and Jake to notice what their father had done out there. About ten seconds, as it happened.

'What's that?'

'Jungle Jim, Jungle Jim!'

They burst out through the back door. With a resigned shrug, Phoebe followed hard on their heels. It wasn't as though she had any choice in the matter.

Confronted with the sight of their father, however, the boys skidded to a halt and positioned themselves behind Phoebe's bare legs. Well, she couldn't help it if they automatically gravitated to the caregiver figure in their lives. *It's part of the job, just like having to accept slimy, half-eaten sweets the first time they make up their minds to be nice and share.*

42

Phoebe glanced at Max and, for one short moment, was certain she saw stark pain in his eyes at his sons' abrupt withdrawal. Then he spoke, and she wondered if she had imagined it.

'Hello.' He scooped up a hammer from the ground and replaced it in the toolbox without really looking directly at either child. 'I got this jungle gym for you both. I hope you enjoy it.'

Max didn't look at Phoebe at all, which was absolutely for the best. So why on earth did she feel disappointed?

Because you're a madwoman, that's why. A total, absolute madwoman with a crush on a man who is so not right for you.

Did she have a crush, even after all her determination to eradicate her recent reactions to him from her system? Probably. How else could she explain her continued overactive interest in him, even in the face of its complete unsuitability?

Please try to focus on the reason you're here. It's a job, remember? Clocking in, clocking out.

Right. The boys remained behind Phoebe's legs. What would an absolutely mega nanny do right now?

Get them to show an interest, she decided. Anything would be a start. She was about to suggest they thank their father for his gift, which would at least be better than no conversation at all, when both boys launched out from behind her, transferring their grip to their father's legs.

'Thank you, Daddy.' Josh gave Max a big squeeze, then let go and hurried over to the gym to inspect it. 'I like it.'

Phoebe's heart squeezed right along with Josh's actions.

Jake stayed longer with his little arms wrapped hard around Max's knees. Just clinging. Then he looked up into his father's face, his expression both serious and hopeful. 'Can we keep it? Are we staying here?'

Oh, Lord. So much for holding back. Phoebe was right in

there with Jake, longing for Max to respond in just the right way. Her heart went out to the little boy. *Pick him up, Max. Take him in your arms and tell him how much you want him, and that you'll never let him go. Let him have the security of knowing somebody loves him and intends to take care of him.*

'You can keep it.' Max's voice was gruff. 'Nobody's going to take it away from you.' He patted Jake's head, then deliberately stepped back, breaking contact.

When disappointment stabbed through Phoebe, she realised just how much she had wanted Max to offer something more than that. To show more care for his sons than he had. To be better than *her* parents had been.

Fortunately, Jake didn't seem to notice anything amiss. 'I'm getting on it.' He started to follow his brother, then paused to look at Phoebe. 'You, too.'

Phoebe forced a smile. 'Okay. I'll give it a go.' She stepped over to the gym. 'Right. What will I try first?' Her question was deliberately hearty, and slowly the burning ache inside her chest began to ease. 'Hmm. Should I climb it? Go up inside? Swoosh through the tunnel?'

She made a production of pretending to wedge herself into the tunnel. 'Oh, dear. I can't seem to fit.' She wiggled her bottom in the air to emphasise the point.

The boys giggled.

'You're too big.'

'Yeah, it fits us, silly.'

'Oh. Then I guess you'd both better show me what you can do on it.' Phoebe gave one final butt wiggle for good measure, but it backlashed a bit when Max issued a strangled groan that sent shivers through all of Phoebe's reactionary sensors.

Phoebe's head whipped up, cracking against the top of the tunnel. Face on fire, other body parts clamouring to follow suit, she backed out.

The moment she straightened up, Max pinned her in place with his gaze. 'About last night.'

Yup. That would be the one subject she really wanted to discuss above all others. Not.

'Forget it.' She shrugged her shoulders in a dismissive gesture, reminded herself that her nose wouldn't actually grow if she told a tall one, and proceeded to do so. 'I promise you, I already have.'

Max hadn't meant anything by it, after all. 'I *do* want to talk about your sons, though.'

She issued the challenge in a quiet tone, lest Jake and Josh should hear her. 'You should have made it clear to them that they don't need to worry about their futures. That you love them, and will look after them properly.'

'They will be looked after.' Max moved away from the gym equipment. 'That's the whole point of getting a good nanny.'

'A nanny is only an employee.' Sometimes the truth hurt. 'Your sons need the unconditional love of the person who created them. That's you, Max. Refusing to commit emotionally to them is as bad as deserting them in reality.'

'Don't question what you don't understand, Phoebe.' Max gestured for her to follow him further away from the play equipment. 'I thought I'd made it clear that you need to keep your opinions to yourself on that whole subject.'

She followed him, her gaze locked on the movement of his long legs, her thoughts tangled in what she wanted for the boys, in the distance she needed to maintain for herself. And in her awareness of Max. 'I'm not sure that I *can* leave the subject alone.'

'Try.' Impatience laced Max's tone. 'And see if you can get your mind focused on this, will you? I've asked Brent to organise a load of sand for the boys as well. I had hoped you'd have some suggestions on the best position for the sandpit.'

Phoebe considered forcing the conversation back to the topic of the boys, then decided she would leave it. For now. Live to fight another day and all that. She'd had about enough, anyway.

'Close to the gym would be good, so both areas can be watched at the same time.' As she spoke, she heard a truck approaching.

Max heard it too and gave a single sharp nod. 'You can tell Brent where to unload. I'm going to take the opportunity to do some work in my study. I'd prefer not to be disturbed.'

Phoebe's hackles reared up. 'What about spending time with your sons?'

But Max either didn't hear as he strode away or pretended not to have done so. Phoebe was left standing there, fuming inwardly, wishing things could be different, feeling disappointed and wanting to shake some sense into Max's stubborn head, all at once.

'Where's the sandpit?' Josh wanted to know.

'Look at the truck. Big truck,' Jake piped up.

Okay, deep breath. Don't spoil this fun moment for them just because you're mad at their father.

Remember you're here for the boys. Do your best for them and you really will have done a top job.

She may be here temporarily, but she had come here to kick butt, rescue-wise. That hadn't changed. She just wanted to kick Max's butt now too. In reality. Even if it was a really nice butt.

And, hey, if Max did find a new nanny Phoebe could always just hang around longer, anyway. Keep an eye on things. It would never work, but she decided to go with the theoretical possibility for now. Since she didn't have any better ideas.

'Okay, guys. Can either of you guess what Brent the gardener has brought along for you?'

Phoebe didn't even bother to mention that the sandpit had

been their father's idea. Let him tell them himself, if he could be bothered to make the time to do so.

Once the boys realised what this next new enterprise was about and immersed themselves in the process of making their sandpit happen, Phoebe managed to calm down a bit.

Enough, at least, that she was able to supervise their exuberance and get to know Brent a little as the young gardener unloaded the river sand in the area she indicated.

Although he conversed easily and had an adult appearance and air about him, he seemed a little shy. When he mentioned he had finished school at the end of last year, she noted the provisional licence plates on the truck and realised why. Despite his grown-up looks, Brent couldn't have been more than eighteen. 'So, Brent, do you have family around here? Brothers, sisters? Parents?'

The gardener seemed quite happy to talk about his family, most of whom lived in or around Sydney. Phoebe nodded and listened, using the time to try to pull herself into a less aggravated frame of mind. Trust Max to rile her.

'They can probably get into the sand now.' Brent's words cut through her thoughts, and she turned to see that the load of sand was indeed sitting there, just crying out for a couple of small people to get in amongst it and make a mess.

'Did you hear that, boys?' She smiled at Jake and Josh, who were hopping from foot to foot, looking hopeful and about ready to burst with unexpended energy. 'You can play in the sand now.'

They each let out a whoop and hurled themselves forward. Stomping seemed to be the order of the day. Phoebe laughed; she couldn't help it. In fact, they were having such a lot of fun that she decided to join them, and soon had her bare feet buried in the cool, moist grains too.

Brent took the truck away and went about some other business. No sooner had he gone than two cars followed each other up the lane. Phoebe moved to the edge of the pile of sand, frowning. Who were they, and what did they want?

Max came out of the house and headed her way, so she supposed the visit must be something he had arranged.

'Good. They're here.' He came to stand close to her as he waited for the vehicles to come to a stop.

He probably hadn't meant to crowd into Phoebe's space, but she felt his presence keenly. It took all her determination not to move away, to put some extra distance between them.

When she glanced up at him, she noted that there were lines of tension bracketed around his mouth. Would they stay uneasy like this with each other, now that she had audaciously suggested he do the right thing and make like a real parent?

The tension had a sensual edge as well. Where the warm day had seemed relaxing and calming for the last few minutes, the heat of Max beside her had a very different effect. She had a compelling urge to run one of her sand-gritted feet the length of Max's shapely calf. And wasn't that just a great way to feel, in the circumstances?

A sound escaped her. It was half groan, half gasp, and she glanced hurriedly at Max to see if he had noticed.

His gaze rested on her, intent and unreadable, then he surprised her and held out a hand. 'Come on, Nanny Phoebe.' His tone was careful, controlled. 'You'd better brush yourself off so you can inspect the merchandise.'

'Wh-what?' For a moment she thought he was inviting her to inspect *him*, even though his very attitude should have convinced her that that was unlikely. Then she realised that he was gesturing towards the small car that had followed the first one in.

Confusion and embarrassment swept over her, but she clasped his hand long enough to balance herself while brushing the majority of the sand from first one foot, then the other. Taking that outstretched hand was a matter of pride. She couldn't let Max know how deeply he affected her. That didn't prevent her body from tingling all over at the slight contact with his, though.

Dratted hormones. *You're just another female to him. Can't you get that into your head?* Sadly, it wasn't her head that was having a whole lot of the problem. 'What about the boys? Shall I get them to come with us?'

'No. We'll be in plain sight. They might as well stay where they are.'

Right. Phoebe let go of Max's hand and put some distance between them. It didn't last, though, because a moment later Max had his hand against the small of her back, guiding her towards the cars—and towards the two men who stood beside the cars, grinning.

'What's all this about?' She gestured at the small car, which seemed to be the focus of Max's attention.

It was a tiny vehicle, for all that it possessed four doors and was a hatchback. The paintwork was faded and had probably once been fire-engine red. At least that was the impression she got from the bits of it that weren't dented or scratched. And the car had cute little headlights that looked like bug eyes. Phoebe thought it was kind of lovable.

'Give me a minute and I'll explain.'

'Okay.' Was Max a little red around the neck and ears? Was that a flush across his cheekbones? Before Phoebe had a chance to decide, he stepped away from her. After exchanging a few words with the men, he shook hands with both and stood back to give them space as they drove away together in the larger vehicle.

In the silence that followed, the sounds of the boys' happy play in the sandpit barely impinged on Phoebe's consciousness. What was all this about?

'Come here, Phoebe.' Max opened the driver's door of the car and gestured for her to get in. 'Take a seat. See what it feels like.'

Phoebe climbed in and felt the old hominess of the car wrap

around her. Despite her determination not to be distracted, she stroked the steering wheel gently. What fun this would be to drive. It was small enough to park on a postage stamp. The turning circle would be brilliant.

She could drive small cars. Really, really well, in fact, as she had proved when she had hired one in a rare bout of financial prosperity and had taken it out on the road. It was only the big vehicles that seemed to get her in trouble.

When Max eased himself into the passenger seat, she turned to face him, questions hovering on her lips, tension sharp against her spine. The sight of him with his knees up around his armpits cudgelled a laugh out of her instead. 'Oh, Max. You look ridiculous.'

'Thank you.' He spoke sarcastically, but without anger, and pulled the door shut, cocooning them in silence.

Through the windscreen she could still see the boys, but they seemed to be in some other, distant world. She and Max were in this one, and it was filled with the scent of old car and Max's sun-warmed skin.

If she leaned just a few centimetres to the left their shoulders would brush, and she wanted that tactile contact more than she should. All Max's fault, she told herself, for kissing her last night.

'Try out the controls. Have a good look at everything.' Max's gruff words broke her reverie and she obeyed mindlessly, testing indicators and windscreen wipers before latching on to the automatic gear lever and moving it from Park to Drive and back again. What was wrong with her, anyway? *Max* wasn't sitting here in the car, panting for a touch of *her*.

'Simple, isn't it?' Max leaned over, maybe to say something more.

Phoebe would never know, because she moved the gear lever again and gasped when her movement brought her hand into contact with a firm muscled thigh. She drew back as though stung, and her gaze flew to his face. His jaw was clenched into a tight line.

'It's a nice car, I'm sure,' she babbled, 'but I don't understand what you're doing with it, nor why you wanted me to see it.'

He searched her face for a moment, then shook his head. 'It's simple. You need to be able to get around while you're caring for my sons. This will make it easy.'

For what? All of a week? But, of course, whoever replaced her would also need to get around. Phoebe reminded herself that Max wouldn't have cared less whether she herself fell in love with the car's little bug eyes or not. It was merely coincidence that he had chosen a car she happened to adore. 'I'm sure the car will be useful. Where did you find it?'

'The Matthews are new neighbours of mine. They bought the Connelly farm. I noticed the car when they first moved in and thought of...' He trailed off and cleared his throat. 'And thought of it today, when I realised it would come in handy. It was a very cheap car.' Max's lower lip jutted and his brows drew down into a vee. 'I got a bargain on it.'

'Bottom of the line in the tin-can range?' Despite herself, Phoebe's mouth turned up into a grin. 'How'd you get it organised so fast?'

'The very bottom.' Max's mouth kicked up too. 'And all it took was a phone call. They're good blokes. We help each other out when we can.'

'Don't you think it's a bit ludicrous?' she asked. When Max's eyebrows simply rose in question, she waved a hand to indicate the beaten-up little car.

'Even taking the nanny angle into consideration, you would never choose this as a second car. Sooner or later you would want to either drive it or ride in it, and you can barely fold yourself up inside it. You should get something bigger that will be more suitable all round.'

'Katherine can drive it too, any time she's here. She's between cars at the moment.' He shifted his legs with blithe unconcern, even though one of them brushed against her own bare skin as a result.

Phoebe tried not to think about the feel of Max's hair-roughened leg against her smooth one. It wasn't easy to dismiss the sensations, yet to move her leg away would seem as though she was making too much of the casual contact.

'Katherine favours large cars too, remember?' She gave up the struggle and moved her leg, only to become further aware of Max's closeness as he reached across her to toy with the knobs on the instrumentation panel. 'She, um, she would never drive something like this.'

Max adjusted the trip meter back to zero, nodded and finally sat back on his side of the car. 'Then I guess you'll just have to accept what I said in the first place. The car will help you to look after my sons. When you're gone it will help the next nanny, and that's why I got it.'

'All right.' What else could she say? 'I'll do my best not to kill it before it's time to hand it over to someone else.'

'Good.' Max climbed out of the car while she was still fumbling with her door catch. 'I'll join you and the boys for lunch,' he tossed over his shoulder as he strode away. 'Until then, I'll be working.'

'And I'll be out here, playing and doing nothing,' Phoebe grumbled under her breath.

Days passed. Max missed his office. He wanted to be in Sydney, clinching deals, wining and dining potential new clients. He wanted to feel as though he had some control over at least one area of his life, damn it.

But even his office staff seemed to be stacked against him. The trouble was that they were so well trained; they were discovering they could function just fine without him. If Max wanted to, he could drop back to simply attending board meetings once a fortnight and the business would go on flourishing without him. Indefinitely.

This knowledge made Max extremely uncomfortable. At least he still had the Danvers project in his hands. He supposed that was something, although with Felicity Danvers chasing him like a bloodhound on the scent—and Max wasn't talking about business here—it wasn't exactly an enjoyable situation.

All Max wanted was entrée into Danvers's international stores, a nice addition to the local business they had already signed over to him. Unfortunately, Felicity seemed to have other ideas.

Her agenda was one Max had seen before. She wanted Max's bank balance and the added prestige associated with his business and his name. She wouldn't be getting either, a fact she would be forced to accept in the end.

Dating Felicity had been a mistake, which was why Max had stopped after two dinners. Well, she would get the message eventually. Max dismissed her from his mind and decided to seek out his sons and their nanny.

For the most part he tried to keep away from them, and that was smart on all counts. There was no point trying to build relationships with his sons when he would simply let them down sooner or later. It was far better not to raise their hopes in the first place, but he had to keep a bit of an eye on them.

As for Phoebe, well, he should have replaced her before now and couldn't understand why he hadn't made more of an effort to do so. It was easy to blame it on not wanting to disrupt the boys further, but they were going to be disrupted when the change happened, no matter how long he put it off.

Surely he didn't *want* to keep Phoebe here? Not when her presence did nothing but stir him up, in every way there was. He wanted her physically. That hadn't gone away, even though he tried to ignore it. And she still annoyed him.

Max made a grumbling sound in the back of his throat and rounded the side of the house.

The scene that met his gaze was registered in a split second. A sprinkler in the centre of the lawn, the fine sunlight turning its spray all the colours of the rainbow. His sons, giggling, dancing around, miniature water pistols clasped in chubby hands.

And Phoebe, clad in the most garish, tasteless bikini Max had ever seen, cavorting on the lawn while his gardener looked on, smiling lecherously whilst pretending to attend to the trellising of a climbing rose nearby.

Working. Hah. Brent was openly ogling the nanny. Just look at that besotted, admiring grin. No wonder. She was all… Max's mind baulked at forming words to describe the effect of long tanned legs, acres of bare mid-section and breasts and hips curved just so to make a man's hands itch to touch and caress.

She also looked at home, here in his garden. As though she belonged, had sprouted here and was meant to stay. What a strange, ridiculous thought. He had no idea what had provoked it. He knew what was provoking the rest of him, though.

'What do you think you're doing?' His question, barked in a loud and accusatory tone, brought instant silence to the entire group although it had been directed only at Phoebe. He glared hard in her direction. 'Have you no sense of moral conduct?'

Brent's eyebrows went up, then he hastily grabbed his working tools and hurried away, mumbling some excuse about needing something from the shed.

Max's sons stared at their father with solemn faces, water pistols resting now in limp, uncertain hands. They looked as though they would like to run away too, but didn't quite dare try it.

'He didn't mean you, darlings.' Phoebe's gentle tone

washed into the uneasy chasm. 'If you like, you can take your guns and squirt water on all the plants you can see. They need help to keep going in this warm weather.'

His sons nodded solemnly and moved away to squirt the rhododendrons beside the veranda.

Once the boys were out of range, Phoebe whirled on Max, her hands on her hips in a provocative manner that made her skimpy covering seem all the more minute.

'What was all that about?' Accusation thrummed through her low words. 'You practically frightened them to death with your growling.'

Max felt like a heel, but whose fault was it that he had been compelled to growl? 'My question wasn't aimed at my sons, as you very well know; it was aimed at you. I've never seen such an appalling display in my life, and I hope I never have to see anything like it again.'

'You accused me of having no sense of moral conduct. I'm afraid you're going to have to explain that.' She picked up the sprinkler and moved it to a patch of grass close by him, spraying him liberally in the process. 'I wasn't doing a dratted thing,' she added, 'other than helping your sons to enjoy themselves on a hot, otherwise uncomfortable, day.'

Max grabbed her arm and tugged her away from the spray. Her blatant understatement of the realities of the situation made his temper boil. He had enough restraint to keep his tone low, but that was all.

'You were cavorting,' he said. 'On the lawn, all but naked, with the gardener, in front of my sons. I don't call that not doing anything.'

'Cavorting?' Her eyebrows hit her hairline. She leaned forward, pushing her face into his space, and giving him a direct view of her cleavage in the process. 'With Brent? As in flinging myself around in a sexual manner? That's what you meant, wasn't it?'

She didn't wait for him to confirm it, only rushed on. 'Are

you just plain blind, Max, or are you sick in the head as well? Do you need medical treatment? Because that's the only reasonable explanation I can think of for you coming at me with such a load of rot.'

'You were setting a bad example in front of my children.' Max's attention strayed over her scantily-clad body again, only this time the perusal was less than speedy. The bikini was a floral design and the flowers were big, one per side of her chest, with a stamen right where—

'That bikini is indecent, and your behaviour in it was also indecent.' He forced his attention upward, to a pair of pouty lips set in an angry pixie face. His breath caught in his throat and he realised he still had hold of her arm. 'You were flaunting yourself in front of the hired help, and doing it with my innocent sons looking on.'

If it occurred to him that this surge of protectiveness towards his offspring was a little out of place with his determination to stay clear of them, he pushed the thought aside. He had other issues on his mind right now.

Phoebe laughed, but it wasn't an amused laugh, and she tugged her arm from his grip at the same time. 'First of all, Max, there is absolutely nothing wrong with my attire. I've seen girls wearing things far more scanty than this.'

When he scowled and made to speak, she held up a hand.

'No. Let me finish.' She waved a hand at her front, encouraging him to look at it. 'See this fabric? It's as thick as a woollen blanket.'

As if being forced to look *there* again wasn't enough to reduce Max's back molars to stubs, she indicated her lower half. 'See the cut, Max? See how it covers more than a pair of granny's underpants would? This bikini is a genuine retro article that's at least three decades old. It would be laughed off any self-respecting beach in the state. It's more decent than a mini skirt and tube top, and plenty of women wear those, *in public*, wherever and whenever they want. And nobody says a thing about it.'

'Uh.' Now that he looked, he saw that what she said was true. Trust Phoebe to find a bikini that would have been perfectly acceptable on a children's TV show, although he stood by his convictions regarding the issue of flower placement.

How had he managed to miss the other pertinent facts? How had she looked so devastating in it, so voluptuous and wanton and hot?

'I apologise.' The words didn't come easy and something, some foolishness or lack of reason, propelled him forward until he could see a rivulet of droplets tracking slowly down into the cleft between her breasts. His finger stopped the flow before his brain registered the decision to do so.

He drew back instantly, stunned by his own behaviour, by her shocked gasp, and by the way his body reacted so immediately and comprehensively to his touching her there. 'Regardless of the actual parameters of your attire, you were still flaunting yourself in it. I'd appreciate it if you didn't try to tempt Brent that way again.' *Or me.* 'So, in future I'd prefer it if you'd wear something a bit more sensible while you're playing water games with my sons.'

'Certainly.' She nodded, two angry splotches of colour riding high on her cheekbones. 'I'll rush into town and get myself a neck-to-ankle ensemble the first chance I have. Would you like that with a swimming cap as well, or is my hair unappealing enough already that it's not likely to inspire the lust of any man within shouting distance of me?'

'Now you're being ridiculous.' Max felt a sense of being ridiculous himself. She was making him feel bad when he had every right to be angry with her. She *had* been playing on the lawn without enough clothes on. If it had affected *him* so thoroughly, every man on the planet would be bound to feel the same way.

'Ridiculous, Max?' Phoebe stuck her nose in the air and

turned aside. 'There's an interesting word. Maybe you should ponder the meaning of it yourself, some time.'

With that, she stalked across the lawn as only Phoebe in bare feet and an ugly, old-fashioned floral bikini could do.

Max released a pent-up growl, but couldn't seem to remove his gaze from the provocative sway of her receding rump. Make that receding, *delectable* rump.

And she *had* been flaunting. Rump included. Max knew what he had seen.

CHAPTER FIVE

'WHAT are you doing?'

'Getting the boys ready to leave the house.' Phoebe glanced once over her shoulder, then turned her attention back to tying Jake's second shoelace into a double knot.

If she continued to look at Max she might be tempted to clock him one, and where would that get them except into more trouble? 'What does it look like I'm doing?'

'You haven't mentioned an outing.'

Disapproval radiated from Max's tone. She didn't have to look at him to hear it, nor to imagine the nasty expression he would be wearing. Her anger over the bikini incident festered back to full life, not that she had managed to subdue it much in the last twenty-four hours, but she *had* tried. A little. Between bursts of cerebral Max-bashing.

She tied the lace, instructed Jake to visit the loo—Josh had been already and was now playing in the boys' bedroom— and smiled benevolently at Max. In a dark-angel sort of way. Or so she liked to imagine.

'I didn't mention an outing?' She fluttered her lashes, just because she knew it would annoy him. 'Gosh, I wonder how I could have overlooked that. I guess I'd better tell you all about it now.'

'In your own time.' Max's eyes were narrowed on her, his jaw clamped into an uncompromising vice. 'I wouldn't want to rush you, or interfere with your schedule, if you even understand the concept of such a thing.'

'Schedules have their place.' She snapped the words. Really, did the man think she existed in a complete vacuum? Did he think caring for children, organising meal times and

59

nap times and all sorts of additional things, involved anything other than good scheduling ability?

'Just because I don't always run to a written timetable doesn't mean I don't have any idea what I'm doing. A person can keep those kinds of plans in their head, you know.'

Max's glance hovered at the top of her head. He snorted. 'In your case I suspect attempting to do so could be quite dangerous.'

'Careful.' Did he have to look at her like that? What was the big attraction with her hair, anyway? She had restrained it as best she could. She forced a smile even though she didn't feel like it. 'Your prejudice towards me is showing.'

'I am *not* prejudiced towards you.'

Not prejudiced, huh? The disparaging twist of his lips said otherwise. Phoebe jutted one hip forward and stuck her fist on it. 'Whilst living with their mother, your sons used to attend daycare. You'd be aware of this, yes?'

'No.' He didn't even apologise for not knowing.

Phoebe felt a burst of indignation on the boys' behalf. *Careful, careful. Stick to the issue at hand.*

'Well, they tell me they did. I'm taking them to visit a daycare centre located at Wentworth Falls that sounds promising.' She glared, silently challenging him. 'You did purchase a car so I could get around with them.'

'A daycare centre? Promising for what?' If there had been anything even remotely relaxed about Max's stance, it disappeared quickly. He unfolded his arms and stepped forward in one swift motion that brought them face to face at a distance that Phoebe couldn't find entirely comfortable.

Oh, all right, then. He was so close she could touch him and, despite everything—and this was what made her so thoroughly annoyed—a part of her *wanted* to touch him.

So, fine. Where Max was concerned she suffered occasional intermittent bouts of, um, well, desire mixed with slight insanity, she supposed would describe it well enough. And could she help it if she suddenly had a thing about shoulders, and that Max's just happened to fit the bill for her thing?

'Promising as a new daycare for them to attend.' She despised the distraction of her thoughts and gave him a good glare to make up for her lapse. 'Boys like Jake and Josh need mental stimulation. Lots of it. Daycare will be a good prelude to more formal education later on.' She waved a hand. 'I'm sure you get the idea.'

'No,' Max said and turned away.

In a moment he would have left the room. Did he really think *no* was an adequate way to discuss this issue?

'Wait.' Phoebe had to restrain herself from grabbing at his arm. Instead, she chewed her lip and waited for him to turn around. When he did, she fired at him again. 'What do you mean, no?'

'I mean *no* to this afternoon's outing, and *no* to daycare. When they have to go to school, they'll go. They don't need anything else before then.' He drew a deep breath and hissed most of it back out in one long, expressive huff. 'There's enough to worry about already without—'

'You can't deny them this.' Max was saying no to the boys going to daycare. What was wrong with him? Phoebe couldn't believe he would simply turn around and veto such a beneficial plan for his sons.

The possibility left her spluttering. 'I've already told them. They're quite excited. Daycare is the one thing they had with their mother that gave them a sense of stability, and that they can carry through now—'

'I don't care what they had with their mother.'

She gasped.

He pinched his lips together and raised his gaze to the ceiling, as though calling for divine intervention. 'What I mean is, I'm in charge of them now. Naturally they need a certain amount of input.'

'Exactly.' This was more like it. 'They need input. Starting with a good daycare where they can meet other kids their own age. I thought you'd jump at the idea of something that would occupy them two days a week.'

Maybe Max was just trying to yank her chain. To make her beg for this concession, when all along it was exactly what he wanted. Yet it didn't look as though that was what he was thinking.

'They may need input,' Max said, glaring at the interruption. 'But that's the idea of a full-time nanny. It's supposed to be the nanny's job to ensure that their minds are developed, that they get enough healthy play and all that sort of thing.'

That perhaps explained one aspect of this. Whether the boys went to daycare or not wouldn't actually impact on Max. Not with a nanny taking care of them twenty-four seven. She wondered where he thought he would find this paragon, and whether it had occurred to him that even paragons didn't work around the clock without occasionally needing to be relieved for small, insignificant reasons, like sleeping.

'A nanny can only do so much.' She caught the sound of small feet in the corridor and hurried on, hoping to get this over with before Jake and Josh entered the room. 'Your sons need organised play among their contemporaries, and they need to be able to trust others to look after them from time to time. Ask any childcare professional. They'll tell you that a good daycare can work wonders for children this age. They get to know their teachers and, next thing you know, they're confiding in them, sharing their secrets, their little concerns, all that sort of stuff.'

'I say it again. They'll have their nanny to confide in. They don't need others to look after them, or to listen to their secrets.' Max's brow looked thunderous, and he cast the full weight of that scowl at Phoebe as he went on. 'As for the rest, invite some other children over to play if you insist. There must be a few of them around this area, and it will achieve the same thing.'

'It *won't*. You see, the memories that Jake and Josh have of daycare are special to them.' The boys had abandoned the corridor and returned to the bedroom, distracted by something or other, but she kept her voice down just in case. Given how angry she felt, it wasn't easy. 'But obviously you don't care about that. For some reason, you've decided they have to miss out on all the opportunities they should have. You're certainly full of surprises, Max. First you don't want them around, then you don't want them to have any fun, either.' She couldn't seem to stop the words, which gained intensity as she went along. 'They're your sons. You're supposed to love them. And when you love people, Max, you have to let them find themselves, *be* themselves, even if that means letting them go out and explore on their own.'

This passionate declaration came straight from her heart, and it was about her as well as his boys, and about the way Max had always butted up against her individuality.

'I know that.' Max snapped the answer, then fell silent. Into that silence the boys rushed, their eyes sparkling as they jumped up and down, yelling their excitement about the proposed trip.

Max looked at his sons, then glared at Phoebe, jaw clenched, eyes shooting angry sparks. 'A visit. I'll agree to that and nothing more.'

Relief swamped her. *For the boys' sakes*. 'You can rest assured, I'll assess the facility thoroughly.'

Clasping a child with each hand, she started for the door, unwilling to linger and give Max time to protest. 'You'll have a full report. If it's not up to standard, I'll admit it immediately and we can—'

'No. *I'll* inspect it.' He took his sons very deliberately from her hold and lifted them, one on to each hip. 'Now, let's get this nonsense over with before I lose my patience completely.'

He didn't notice that he had reached out voluntarily to his sons. Nor that they had accepted that blunt protectiveness without question. Phoebe told herself not to pin any hope on one small sign, given in anger, for goodness' sake, and forced her thoughts elsewhere.

The daycare centre backed on to natural bushland. Max parked the car in one of the bays and climbed out to assess the view of the converted house while Phoebe did some last-minute fussing over his sons. As though they had to be made to look good enough.

The resentful thought crept up on him in much the same way his earlier protectiveness had done. And look where that had led him. Straight into trouble, in the form of this visit. For someone determined to steer clear of messing up his sons' lives, he wasn't doing much of a job of staying out of things.

He was their father, though, which meant he had to make various decisions on their behalf. He had made decisions for Katherine too. It had only been when he had tried to get close personally that the problems had arisen.

So, right. Organising—check. Planning and considering and decision-making—check. Messing them up by trying to be too personally involved—uncheck.

'Let's go.' He growled the words, determined to get this fiasco over with as quickly and painlessly as possible. 'If I'm going to look this place over I can't assess much, standing here in the car park.'

'On the contrary, *we* can assess a great deal from right here.' Despite the wide smile she turned on him, her eyes flashed fire. Blue was supposed to be a cool colour, but Phoebe's eyes were anything but. Instead, they were full of challenge and determination. The woman was stubborn to the bone.

'Like what?' he asked. 'The way the paintwork blends in with the skyline?'

'Accessibility. Parking facilities. Surroundings.' She gritted the words out, then turned to his sons, plastered a smile on her face and deliberately included them in the conversation. 'Isn't it lovely? All that bushland behind, just like at home.'

'We like our new house,' Jake chirped.

'We live there now,' Josh added.

'The play equipment looks good. Sensible. Sturdy. Plenty of room and plenty of variety.' Phoebe's gaze rested on the large play yard. She had his sons at her side, one small hand held in each of hers.

Why those feminine hands should appear so capable at this instant was a mystery to Max. The sudden urge to feel them on his body was easier to explain, albeit unwelcome. He was almost getting used to wanting Phoebe, which was probably even more dangerous than wanting her in the first place.

'Most of the materials in that yard are wooden.' He strode along reluctantly at her side as she headed towards the entrance of the daycare centre. As they drew nearer, he gestured towards the largest thing he could see, a fort-like structure with a small rung ladder leading up on one side, a ramp on the other. 'That fort looks positively unsafe. It's far too high off the ground, for starters.'

'Not really, and think how much fun a little boy would have up there, pretending to be a soldier on the lookout for the enemy.'

'War games are not appropriate.'

'I meant from a historical perspective,' she said, 'and, besides, imagination is a joy.' The yellow bow in her hair bobbed as she bounced contrarily towards the daycare's entry door. 'It should be encouraged.'

She seemed determined to barge into the place in full sail, but Max had no intention of trailing in the wake of this particular ship.

'Allow me to get the door for you,' he said, and forced his way to the front.

They entered as a tight bunch, and Max paused to look around. The place was a visual blast of colour. On the walls, the floors, in paintings and curtains. Red, blue and yellow everywhere and, splashed among them, bright greens and oranges and purples and pinks.

The centre also vibrated with noise. How anyone could possibly have noticed their arrival, Max couldn't imagine, but a middle-aged woman bustled out of a room full of children and met them in the foyer. Max braced himself to greet her coolly.

'You must be Phoebe.' Ignoring him, the woman leaned past him and stretched out a hand.

Phoebe smiled and grasped it. 'Carol? Thanks for fitting us in today. The boys are very excited to be here.'

She introduced Josh first, then Jake, and finally Max, as though he mattered least of all. Max gritted a greeting and wondered how many minutes it would be before they were all back in the car, leaving.

'Let's show them around.' The woman—Carol—strode off as though she simply expected everyone to follow.

Max didn't like managing women. Maybe, he thought snarkily, this explained Phoebe's deep interest in childcare. The vocation would suit her overbearing, bossy personality to a T. Drawing an irritated breath, Max followed into the fray.

Only to get distracted. By Phoebe. Of course.

The problem was, she had the most mouldable bottom. Two perfect globes, begging for the caress of appreciative hands. And those globes were undulating from side to side in front of him right now in the most distracting manner. This was another perfect example of why he should have stayed locked up in his study, even if there wasn't any work to do.

Max wanted her. Phoebe. The stuff his nightmares had been made of for so long. The desire for her hadn't gone away since that mistaken kiss. Hadn't settled down, receded or in any other way lost its power.

For a little while he had managed to ignore it, that was all. But he wanted her right now, in the middle of the daycare centre, despite the crawling mass of small children and the noise and the bustle.

As if that weren't bad enough, in the past few minutes his intellect had turned against him as well, pointing out at every turn the quality and suitability of the facility. Something Phoebe had claimed to know from the first. Josh and Jake were having a ball. That had to count for something too.

And why should Max mind enrolling them, if they were going to enjoy the place and it would give them something to do that didn't involve him in any way?

The argument should have made perfect sense. Max couldn't understand why it left him feeling fed up and somehow disappointed.

'It's a great daycare centre, Max.' Phoebe straightened and swung to face him, belligerence clear in both stance and expression. 'I know you've been standing here judging it for all you're worth, but if you'll just let go of that pigheaded tunnel vision for one minute and—'

'It's a quality concern.' What he had been judging was her bottom, but he wasn't about to say so. And he didn't like her making assumptions about him, even if they may have had an element of truth to them.

Still, Max prided himself on being able to change his point of view on the rare occasion, like now, that he realised he may have made a slightly premature judgement. 'Excellent staff, good organisation.'

There was a certain amount of perverse pleasure to be had in watching her shocked reaction to his volte-face. He planned to enjoy it while it lasted, which, knowing Phoebe, wouldn't be long. 'Jake and Josh clearly like it here. Like the interaction, the structure, the opportunities. I'm prepared to enrol them.'

'You're…you, uh…what's that?' If her mouth fell any further open it would hit the floor.

'I said I'll enrol them. Today, if it can be arranged.'

Phoebe continued to stare at him dumbly. It was the first less than professional exhibition she had given since arriving here.

In fact, she had blended in beautifully with the other day-care leaders. Had moved from small group to small group, keeping an eye on his sons without appearing to obviously do so. Interacting with all the children impartially, seeming to understand each small need, each quirk of nature.

In short, Phoebe was a wonder at this kind of thing. A natural. Max liked her professional expertise. Admired it. Admired her *for* it. Wanted her somehow in a different way, a deeper way, now that he had seen her in action here. None of which was at all good for his peace of mind.

CHAPTER SIX

'I NEVER get tired of looking into that blue haze. It's gorgeous.' Phoebe leaned one arm against the safety rail as she gazed across the Jamison Valley towards the Three Sisters mountain formation and wondered how irritated Max was with her. On a scale of one to ten, would they be talking, say, five? Or fifty-five?

They were at the Queen Victoria Lookout opposite Katoomba Falls, with the mountain panorama spread before them. A deep valley filled with native gums and bushland hummed with the sound of birdsong below. It was a lovely, peaceful spot, but the man at her side didn't appear to be enjoying it particularly, and all thanks to her.

She had suggested a sightseeing expedition after the trip to the daycare centre, to ensure that Max spent some quality time with the boys.

Max stood now, with his sons tucked between him and the guard rail at the lookout and a thundercloud lurking on his brow. He hadn't said much. Had simply glared daggers that promised retribution later. Phoebe refused to feel sorry. Not when the boys were cosied up to their daddy this way. It had to be doing *something* to Max. Well, he wasn't pushing them away and that was a good start.

The boys seemed content for the moment to stare at the view. Jake had his arm wrapped around Max's leg. Phoebe wondered if Max had realised his sons might simply ignore his barriers. Children had a tendency to push past that sort of thing, given half a chance.

'It was good of you to bring them, Max.' She accompanied the words of praise with a generous smile.

'You think you have it all worked out, don't you?' The wind ruffled his hair, giving him a raffish look that was difficult to resist, but she wasn't going to get distracted from her cause. Not this time.

'We should take them on the scenic railway as well.' He wouldn't want to, but since when was she letting that worry her? 'Give them a bit of a thrill. It *is* the best train ride in Australia, after all.'

'No,' Max said quietly. 'You can take them some time by yourself, if you want to do it that much. I'm not stupid, Phoebe. I'm aware you've been pushing me, and why. Now it stops.'

But he hadn't counted on two train-mad boys.

'Please, Daddy. Can we?'

'We like trains.'

The boys started jumping up and down and, a moment later, were running back towards the car. With the trust of the very small, they simply assumed they were going. Phoebe did feel a tad guilty then.

Max glared as they caught up with the boys and guided them safely the rest of the way. 'I won't be manoeuvred, Phoebe. Do you understand?'

'I wasn't.' She stopped abruptly. 'Look, if you don't want to go, that's fine. I'll gladly take them myself, tomorrow.'

After ensuring the boys were strapped in properly, she climbed into the front passenger seat. Her posture was stiff, but she couldn't help it. She had only wanted to make things better for the three of them.

Max took them on the scenic railway in the end, without saying a thing about it. His boys seemed happy in his company, which made Phoebe happy too. There would most likely be hell to pay later, but it would be worth it for this. She threw herself into enjoying it while it lasted.

The railway ride led to ice creams for everyone. Phoebe chose a multi-hued concoction that smelled exactly like berry-

flavoured bubble gum, and smiled when Max pulled a re-
volted face.

He chose Wildberry Delight, which immediately prompted
Phoebe to want to taste it—straight from his tongue.

Great. Just great. And now Max was looking at her with
heat in his eyes and she couldn't think straight. 'The park.'
Her tone held an edge of desperation that she, at least, could
hear. 'Swings and things.'

She should have said that it was time to go home. That
would have been smarter, but then she hadn't been smart today, had she? She waited for Max to say no and blast her for
yet again trying to push him to do something he didn't want
to do.

But Max merely stood and waved a hand towards the car.
'By all means, let's make the day complete and go to the
park.'

It may have started out with Max's sarcastic invitation, but
things happened at the park. Things like the moment when
Max brushed against her hip as he lunged to catch one over-
excited son as he flung himself down the slide with a confidently shrieked, 'Watch me!'

Then there was the second when Phoebe's hand touched
Max's as they both reached out to slow a swing to a safer
speed.

Oh, and the shift in time when she ran full tilt into him
because she was simply laughing too hard with sheer enjoy-
ment of the boys to notice Max's presence as she turned.
Max's arms had closed about her possessively and locked
tight, and he had got the most thoughtful look on his face as
well as a dark awareness in his stormy grey eyes.

Breathless moments later Phoebe had pulled back, convinced her colour must be high. Max had released her, but
the effect of the moment had lingered.

Dusk was falling now as they bundled the exhausted boys
into the back of the four-wheel drive, ready to head for home.

Phoebe turned from fastening Jake into his safety seat. 'All done.'

'Yes.' Max drew back, but not quickly enough.

Their bodies brushed as she backed away from the vehicle. Max moaned and shifted out of range.

Phoebe swung around to face him.

'I want to take you,' he said. 'Home.' The words grated out of him. Double-edged. Exciting. Raw. 'It's late. For my sons. They need their rest.'

Oh, my. *Oh, me, oh, my.*

Phoebe blinked. Shifted her gaze from his face, then back again, unable to stay away from the heat of his look. 'Of course. The sooner they're tucked up for the night, the better.'

And if that wasn't double-edged, too, she didn't know what was, although she hadn't set out to say it that way.

They travelled in silence as darkness fell. Max turned the car's lights on, and Phoebe watched through glimpses in the rear-view mirror as the boys fell asleep within moments of each other, propped in their safety seats in the back.

Phoebe fell into a half doze, in which she dreamed she was still participating in Jake and Josh's lives years from now, and Max was there too, a shadowy but familiar figure in the background.

'Fine how I am,' she mumbled grumpily in her sleep. 'Don't need anyone. Not lonely. Perfectly happy by myself.'

And Max, entertaining his own thoughts, glanced at Phoebe, and wondered...

'If you take Jake, I'll carry Josh. If we transport them both at once, we'll be least likely to have one or both of them wake up.' Phoebe spoke in a hushed, even tone and didn't look directly at Max.

She wasn't stupid. She knew Max had been fighting his attraction to her today. He didn't want that, any more than he really wanted *her* to be the one here helping him with his sons. And when he hadn't been fighting the attraction he had been annoyed at her for trying to manoeuvre him. She would like to avoid any discussion about that, if possible.

She knew the reality. Max didn't want her anywhere near his sons. Not permanently. He had only let her stay this long because he was still in shock and not functioning at his usual forceful and speedy capacity. He'd get his breath back shortly, and then Phoebe would have to leave. She accepted that, but there was no need to go over it tonight, was there?

'Right. Let's go, then.' Max climbed out of the car.

Phoebe followed suit. The air smelled of cool eucalypt leaves and damp loamy soil. The effect should have been calming, but the air also felt close. Still. Stifling. Phoebe shrugged in the darkness. It was probably just anticipation of an altercation with Max choking her.

She dismissed the surroundings and focused on building some sensible short-term goals. She would put the boys to bed and retire herself, happy at least in the knowledge that she had proved Max wrong today. That he had been forced to admit the daycare centre would be good for his sons.

That was something, after all. She would prefer to go to bed on that than on accusations from Max.

She heaved the sleeping Josh into her arms and headed for the house. Max's heavier footsteps echoed close behind her, but she refused to think of those. Instead, she buried her face in soft, little-boy hair and inhaled the scent of shampoo and dirt and hard play.

That was another oops, but too late, now to worry about lack of a bath before bed.

Max entered the house first, leaving her to follow in his wake. To watch in the moon-limned night as he gently settled Jake into the bed, eased his shoes off and turned away.

'I'll just put Josh down—'

'Let me take him—'

They spoke as one. Phoebe moved towards Josh's bed, intending to lower him. Max moved towards Phoebe. Reached for his son and, as he did, his hand touched her breast. Sensual electricity sizzled to immediate life, lighting her nerve-endings, sending her gaze flashing to Max's.

He took Josh. Lowered him into the bed. Kissed him and tucked him in. Performed the same ritual with Jake. Phoebe stood as though turned to stone. A part of her mind screamed at her to leave, but her feet wouldn't move.

When he finished with his second son, Max took her arm just above the elbow and propelled her out of the room, down the corridor, and into the sitting room. She found her coordination again then, pulling away from him, and stood clutching her arms across herself.

The image of him laying his sons to their slumber wouldn't leave her mind. Tenderness had etched his face, easing the hard planes and angles into something else altogether. He had looked almost lonely.

How did this reconcile with Max's determination to stay clear of them? *She. Just. Didn't. Get. It.*

If Max could soften towards his boys, well, the possibilities were limitless. He could love. Want a complete family. The direction of these thoughts scared her. It was time to get out of here. Fast.

'Goodnight,' she muttered almost beneath her breath as her feet edged towards the door. 'It's late and I'm tired and I need my rest so I can be up with the sparrows and two energetic boys at first light.'

'Wait.' The single word arrested her. Max crossed the room, took hold of her arm, turned her and walked to the sofa, pushing her down into it. 'I want to talk to you.'

'To talk.' Exactly what she didn't want, and the way he was looking at her was so odd.

He sat in one of the armchairs, stretched out his long legs and crossed one foot over the other. Relaxed, yet not.

'Yes. Talk,' he said. 'What are your plans for the future? What do you want to do with your life?'

'What's this, Max?' She tried to hold a relaxed posture too. Didn't want him to sense her confusion. Her wariness. 'A lecture on my shiftlessness? Do you plan to reform me with a few well-chosen words? Point out that I could make something of myself if I would just put my mind to it?' She had thought he would attack her pushiness first, but maybe he was saving that for later in the programme.

'I want to know if you're happy the way you are.' Max spread his hands before him. 'If there are other things you want, are determined to have.'

'Why?' What bearing did it have on their situation? On her temporary care of his sons? And why wasn't this shaping up to be the wrangling match Phoebe had predicted?

'I'll explain my reasons, if you'll answer first.'

'All right. What do I want out of my life?' What *did* she want? The thought slipped insidiously into her head, past her guard. She could want Max. Max *and* his two darling boys. For ever, instead of just while Jake and Josh needed a nanny and until Max picked a better one and threw Phoebe out.

'I want the usual things.' She waved a hand, dismissing the depths, bringing it back to surface stuff. 'To be happy, to feel as though I'm contributing somehow. My needs aren't great.'

'What about further education? Your career path? Is there anything specific you'd like to achieve in that sphere?'

Maybe he did plan to lecture her, after all. Oddly, she almost relaxed at the thought, but then she looked at Max to see him watching her so intently. In fact, his gaze was all but eating her. With interest in her answers, but with something else too. Something hot and tightly leashed. The blood thickened in her veins in response to the deeper part of that look.

'Assisting...' She drew a breath, tried to steady herself. 'Assisting at daycare centres is great, but what I'd like, some day, is to get the qualifications to teach in elementary school.'

'Go to uni.'

'Yes. Get a Bachelor of Education.'

'You could do it part time, spread it out to suit the rest of what was happening in your life.'

'I suppose.' What was he getting at? She was more confused now than ever. 'Max, I'm not sure I understand where you're—'

'Marriage. The two of us. It would solve everything.'

'—heading with this. What?' She stared mutely at him and wondered if she was dreaming.

He raked a hand through his hair. 'I'm suggesting we marry. I think it's a good idea.'

Phoebe gaped at him. At staid, upright, sensible Max, who had just asked her, Phoebe Gilbert, abandoned child of an exotic dancer and a politician who didn't want to know about it, to marry him. 'I don't understand.'

For a second her heart hoped. She would belong. With Max and Jake and Josh, here in this house, the four of them together. A family. Oh, wow. She could have everything she had ever wanted. It wouldn't even *matter* that she couldn't have a baby, then. Max was asking her to form a family with him. He thought she was worthy of that. He'd seen something in her that made him believe…

Phoebe wanted to jump up and down with joy. To burst into tears and never stop crying. It was so perfect. So wonderful. So totally unexpected and incredible.

Then Max started talking, leaning forward in his chair with his hands clasped and his gaze fixed on her face. 'There are a lot of advantages, Phoebe. I've examined the idea from all angles, and it makes a lot of sense.'

He sounded so businesslike, and Phoebe knew what that meant. Max was attacking this in the same way he would sit down to work out farm profitability or something. In a cold, uninvolved sort of manner.

Her excitement sagged, and she clamped her lower lip between her teeth, wishing she could stop him right now, clap her hands over her ears and refuse to hear another word. Life never let you off the hook that way, though, so she sat there and tried to look as though she hadn't thought he had just offered her the moon and stars then made her wonder if they were real.

'I'd have permanent care for my sons. You'd be able to get your credentials eventually, without worrying about money.' Max made a gesture to encompass their surroundings. 'You'd have all this.'

Is that it? Is that all you think marriage means? The words were in her throat but they wouldn't come out. She was too busy shrivelling up inside. Going into herself. Tucking it all away where she could agonise over it later on her own. How stupid was she, anyway?

Of course Max wouldn't have wanted her for love. And it wasn't as if she loved him, either. One couldn't love one's enemies, after all, and Max had always been that. Phoebe clung to the thought like a life raft.

'And we'd have good sex.' His gaze darkened, roamed over her possessively. 'The chemistry is there, even if it does surprise me.'

He laughed, at himself, she knew, but it still felt like a slap in the face. Phoebe wanted to tell him she had entertained dozens of lovers and they had all thought she was wonderful. Anything to wipe that confident self-possession from his expression. And she wanted to hurt him some way and scream in his face, but she did none of those things. She just sat there, not speaking, not trusting herself. Hurting.

He spread his hands wide and shrugged. 'I'm attracted to you. You're attracted to me. If we join forces, we both get to have what we want. A good time in bed, a solution to your poverty, a caregiver for my boys. I'm sure you're probably surprised.' He stopped. Shrugged. 'I surprised myself when I first came up with the idea today. But I think it would work.

I think it's really worth a try. I'd never have married anyway so I have nothing…'

To lose. She completed the sentence for him silently. Fortunately, her temper came to her aid before the tears won out. She had been carried away for a moment by a nice little dream that had absolutely no basis in reality, but that moment was past and Phoebe was starting to climb out of her shock enough to think.

Max was no hero. No knight in shining armour. He wasn't even, she decided with a spurt of rage, remotely likeable, when all was said and done.

Fuelled by this very welcome anger, she shot to her feet. He stood too, which brought them closer together. Close enough to touch, although she wouldn't. She didn't trust her self-control that much yet, and there were probably laws against attacking one's employer.

She held her ground, though, and looked up into his face, her own gaze narrowed and filled with all the frustration and scorn that she felt. 'I have never been in a state of *poverty* in my life.'

Out of respect for the children sleeping not so far away, she kept her voice low, but it was no less deadly for that. 'I suppose you thought you'd buy me some further education along the way, in this tidy little marriage plan of yours?'

'Naturally, as your husband, I would—'

'No.' She knew she was avoiding the harshest aspects and focusing on the easiest bits. At least she was doing *something*.

'That side of it isn't even an issue, really.' If he even heard her 'no', he gave no indication of it. Instead, he reached for her. 'This is about us, not about some ephemeral higher education you might never even pursue.'

'So I'm shiftless too now, as well as poverty-stricken. Unable to commit to a task and see it through.' She backed away, just far enough that she was out of range. 'This is only the beginning of what's wrong with your idea.'

He paused, puzzled, let his hands drop to his sides. 'Try to see this from my perspective, rather than colouring it with some bizarre outlook of your own.'

Couldn't he hear himself? Wasn't that enough to show him? To make him realise what a mistake it would be, how stupid he was being, even to think of it? Marriage for all the wrong reasons. Marriage to take care of a sexual itch, and to help him to avoid having to commit deeply to his sons.

Anything else he could have continued having without making any changes to their circumstances at all. He wanted to change *her*. To make her something other than who and what she was, and then, possibly, he might be able to tolerate having her in his life. For the sake of expediency.

'I won't marry you, Max. I don't see a single benefit to such a plan.' She set her lips and squared her shoulders and told herself she would not show, in any way, that he had hurt her. Let the unfeeling twit remain blind.

'I'm not interested in a sexual liaison with you, I don't need your help to escape a financial situation and, although I care about your sons, and *I do*, I admit that, I don't see my role as encompassing being here to cheer them on when they're old and grey and as doddery as you'll be one of these days.'

After a second of staring at her in stunned shock, Max stepped towards her. She was having none of that and flung through the door into the hallway and slammed it shut behind her before he could take another step. She stalked along the corridor and into her room, thudding that door shut too, as forcefully as she could without risking waking the boys.

Marriage, indeed. And he said *she* was the one with the ridiculous ideas.

Phoebe just hoped her anger held up long enough for her battered heart to recuperate somewhat.

CHAPTER SEVEN

'ARE you completely out of your mind?' Max flung the chicken coop door open with such force that half his hens flapped to the far end of the yard in a ruffled, squawking mass. 'This is *not* part of the nanny's job description.'

With each step closer, he found it more difficult to hold on to his temper. What man wouldn't? He had to have the most aggravating temporary nanny on the face of the planet, bar none, and right now she was digging holes all over his chook yard.

'No, it isn't, is it?' Phoebe, pink-gumbooted feet perched atop the shovel, sent it deep into the loamy soil and hovered there, staring at Max for all the world as though *he* was the strange one. 'But then I'm not on duty, so I guess it doesn't really matter.'

'Not on duty?' Max's eyes narrowed into slits. 'Are you saying you quit?'

'No, Max, although you're clearly going to have to replace me. We've known that from the start, and now it's twice as necessary.'

Because of last night? He had thought about that, of course, while he had lain awake trying to figure out how a simple, sensible, uncomplicated marriage proposal could go so spectacularly wrong. While he had tried to come to terms with the fact that he had come up with the perfect plan to fix his problems and Phoebe had scotched it stone cold. While he had wrestled with the cold bite of disappointment that just wouldn't seem to quit.

And while he had considered all those things, he had realised something. Phoebe had him backed into a corner. In her short time here, she had weaselled her way into the boys' hearts so thoroughly that it would be cruel to them if he tried to replace her now.

Irrational? Absolutely not.

And if she thought, in the face of all this, that she could simply walk away, Max had news for her! 'If you leave now it will be because you're too selfish to stay and finish what you started.'

A tightness took hold of his chest as he waited for her response.

'Just exactly what do you mean by that?' She puffed up like an agitated bullfrog. 'Surely, after what happened last night, and the lack of welcome you've displayed since I first got here, you can't possibly now be saying—'

'Nothing happened last night.' He was more familiar with this irritable, reactionary Phoebe, and he slung words at her in much the way he would have in the past. 'I put forward a suggestion. You rejected it. End of story.'

Normally, Phoebe would have stuck her chin out and slung right back at him. Max was ready for that—primed for it. He'd be lying through his teeth, he admitted, because last night had been a whole hell of a lot more than *nothing happened*.

Max didn't make a habit of proposing marriage. In fact, he had believed he would never ever take that step. Yet he had done so with Phoebe and she had rejected his offer, and that knowledge still galled him.

It also galled him that his situation, *because of that marriage proposal and her reaction to it*, was now twice as complicated as it had been beforehand.

He refused to expose any of this to Phoebe, though, and simply shrugged his shoulders. 'I don't see why what happened last night has to make any difference to anything. It was an idea. A foolish one, I admit, now that I've had time to think it through a bit more. But the issue is over with now, forgotten. We, on the other hand, have to move forward. I had assumed you would want to do that in a way that was in the best interests of Jake and Josh. They've come to care for you, so it would be best if you stayed on. But maybe you're not interested in what's best for them any more?'

'No, I...of course I want what's best for the boys.' There was no return fire. No jutting chin. For a moment, he thought he saw a gleam of tears in her eyes. He must have been mistaken, because she tossed her head a second later and jumped up and down on the shovel some more, causing all her body parts to jiggle along.

'What you said about the idea of us getting married is true.' She jumped some more. 'It surprised me to hear you suggest something so stupid, so completely unsuitable, but I guess I can forget about it if you can.'

'Well, good then.' This was the reaction he had anticipated from Phoebe. It put things back on familiar territory and he should have been relieved. He *would be*, just as soon as he'd had time to get his mind adjusted to the alterations to his plans.

No marriage. But he wanted Phoebe to stay on, caring for the boys. Max would go back to work. In another week or so, probably. He hadn't had a holiday in for ever. Now that he was already out of the office, he might as well take one.

He wouldn't go anywhere. He would just relax at home. Do a few odd jobs, maybe, or take a stronger interest in the farm. It had been a while since he had had an actual face to face meeting with his farm manager. He might do that.

Meanwhile, he still had no idea why Phoebe was out here. Why she had abandoned the boys she claimed to care so much about. And he wanted a concrete commitment out of her. *For his sons*, he insisted mentally. 'I want your agreement that you'll stay on indefinitely, caring for my sons on a full-time basis.'

'I'll agree to continue for as long as we both believe it's

working out.' Her nod was very formal, and completely un-smiling.

'I'll expect proper care.' He gestured at their surroundings. 'What are you doing out here when you should have been inside, watching the boys? Why did you leave them in the house when I hadn't even emerged from my room? They could have got up to all kinds of mischief.'

'The only mischief they got up to was forcing you out of bed before you were good and ready to get up.' She flung this at him as though he were a lazy slob.

It was far from the truth. 'I'm not sure this will work, if you're going to do things that make the boys vulnerable.'

'Is that right?' She stamped on the shovel a couple of times. It went deeper into the ground, and Max got a first-hand view of every centimetre of her legs, half her backside and a fair expanse of midriff.

His body responded predictably, which didn't exactly improve his temper. Not being able to slake his physical interest in her was one aspect of his rejected marriage proposal that he had been trying not to think about.

'You've been moaning that you want the best for your sons,' Phoebe said, 'haven't you?'

For a moment, he got stuck on the *you've been moaning* part. Then he managed to put it into context with the rest of what she had said.

'I've made it clear I want the best for them.' He ran a frustrated hand through his hair. What he really wanted to do was run it over her legs and midriff wherever the jeans shorts and abbreviated top allowed. They might be back to sniping at each other, but that didn't stop his body reacting to hers. Damn it to hell. 'What's that got to do with you deserting them this morning?'

'I'm helping you to achieve your goal, while ensuring appropriate working conditions for myself at the same time. You need to give more of yourself to Jake and Josh, Max. They need that from you. This morning, I decided to help you along a bit, that's all.'

He got the bit about forcing him to spend time with his sons. Got it, and got angry about it. Hadn't she understood, yesterday?

Phoebe glanced at the pecking hens and smiled. 'Don't you just love the way they snap those worms right up?'

Had she put a particular emphasis on the word *worms*? Of course she had.

Max whacked the wheat feeder, and got a very juvenile sense of satisfaction when she jumped slightly. 'Just making sure the beady-eyed bats won't go hungry any time soon,' he said blandly.

'Oh!' Phoebe glared daggers at him.

Max stared complacently back. 'Don't try to steer me in your chosen direction again, Phoebe. You're here to perform a role. It doesn't include manipulating things because you think you know better.'

'Fine.' She jumped on the shovel in short, angry bursts of movement. 'Then I suppose that just leaves the other reason for my absence from the house this morning.'

'And what would that be?' Whatever other accusation she had to level at him, Max could hardly wait to hear it so he could refute it. Phoebe had to learn that there were limits. That she couldn't just have whatever she wanted, just because she wanted it.

No doubt it would be some other totally unacceptable family-related demand.

'Time off,' she suggested, with a *Hello? Are you awake in there?* intonation. 'You know? Regular scheduled breaks from the twenty-four hour a day duty of caring for two small boys?' She lurched in preparation for jumping off the shovel.

Without thinking about it, Max lunged forward and caught her. For a long moment she remained poised on the shovel and they were eyeball to eyeball with his hands on her bare middle.

She was soft, incredibly so, and slender. A careless hold would bruise her, but he wasn't being careless. He just couldn't seem to let go. Worse, he wanted to go on exploring her until there was nothing left to discover. Damn her, anyway. For making him want her, then refusing a viable solution which could deal with that wanting.

'You should take care how you get down from that thing.' He set her down and stepped back, divorcing himself from the feel of her, from the enticement of warm, supple skin. And her words sank in. 'You're out here because you're having time off?'

'That's right.' Phoebe took a slow, deep breath, gathered the shovel and walked to the door of the pen. 'I'm finished in here, but if you want to stay—'

'Naturally I don't.' Max stalked out behind her, slid the bolt home on the door, then wondered what to do next. 'It goes without saying that you're entitled to a day off. I simply might have expected—'

'Good. I knew you'd understand. You probably even regret that you overlooked to do anything about arranging time off for me prior to now.'

'You haven't exactly been here for decades, you know.' But just like that, she frustrated him. Put him on the back foot. Made him feel mean-spirited and thoughtless. 'In any case, I apologise. I've been…'

Distracted? Out of my mind with lust for someone I don't even like? Was that latter part true, though, now? He shook his head, sick of the brain drain.

'I've been focused on other things. I didn't think about it. If you like, we can go inside right now and work the details out.'

'Oh, no need.' She shook her head, all airy confidence all of a sudden. Max wanted to snatch her up and kiss her until she admitted that there was something between them, that it hadn't gone away, and that it wouldn't until they allowed it to reach its natural conclusion. One way or the other.

Unaware of his thoughts, she positively smirked with self-righteousness. 'I'm sure now that the issue's been brought to your attention you'll see to it that my working hours aren't too taxing in future.'

'Right. Good. Naturally I'll do that for you.' He gritted his teeth. Maybe he should just forget the marriage and caring for his sons angle, and simply sleep with her. At least that way he might get her out of his system. Kind of like removing an unwanted foreign body from his bloodstream. 'Nice of you to be understanding about the issue of your hours, then,' he got out somehow.

'I'm going to have a brilliant day, as it turns out, because Brent has the day off too. He and I are going to do some stuff together.' Phoebe seemed completely oblivious to Max's thoughts. Perhaps it was as well because, right now, those thoughts were particularly aggressive.

'I sent Brent away with the boys.' *And if I'd known he was going to hit on my nanny, I'd have considered sending him away permanently.* 'He was going into town, so I asked him to take them along for the ride.'

'Forgot it was his day off, huh? At least you gave him one, I suppose, even if you then went on to violate it,' Phoebe pointed out.

'Actually I did forget, or I wouldn't have presumed on him that way.' Despite what Phoebe might think, Max rarely forgot anything and he didn't make a habit of taking advantage of people.

She shrugged and started for the house.

A vehicle emerged on the long driveway. Brent was back. Max told himself it didn't bother him that Phoebe intended to spend the day with the young gardener, but he found it hard to believe himself. 'We have matters to discuss.'

'Oh, whatever it is, I'm sure it'll wait.' She waved cheerily to Brent as he brought the vehicle to a halt over by the sheds. 'I'll send the boys across to you. Bye-ee.'

Phoebe strolled away, pink gumboots slapping against her ankles. Who went any place civilised wearing gumboots? Even if they were pink, rather than the regulation black or orange? And *bye-ee*? Max shoved his fisted hands into the pockets of his shorts and stalked to the veranda. Bye-ee, indeed.

Only then, as his sons crossed the yard towards him, did it hit Max that Phoebe was deserting him to care for them for the whole day. By himself.

She had manipulated him again, and he had let it happen. Had been so absorbed in wanting her, reacting to her, that he hadn't even noticed where it was all going until it was too late.

Despite their previous painful days with him, though, Max fluked a decent time of it with the boys. It was easier with the play equipment and the sand pit. Since Phoebe had used the sprinkler and water guns with good success, Max copied that trick too.

When Josh and Jake got a bit fidgety in the afternoon he took them outside to save the furniture and ended up touring one of the apple orchards, explaining the growth process in great detail, all of which most likely went straight over their small heads.

But they seemed to enjoy kicking at the loose clods in the furrowed rows between the trees, and this would all be theirs one day. He wanted them to have an appreciation for it, if they possibly could. The irony didn't go unnoticed. Teaching his boys to love their inheritance whilst keeping his distance from them.

Max wished it could be different, but he couldn't make himself into something he wasn't. Couldn't give them something that just wasn't there in him to give.

Night crawled in. He put the boys to bed and by then he barely noticed that it was an easy task. His thoughts were with Phoebe, and they stayed there through several more hours until she finally arrived home—by which time Max was royally steamed and spoiling to share it around.

When she slipped in the front door he was waiting for her. 'Had a nice time, have you?' Sarcasm laced his tone. He had more to say. A whole lot more, in fact, like, *It's after midnight. Your day off is officially over. Somewhat irresponsible, don't you think, to stay out so late when you need to be alert to look after my sons in the morning?*

That was her job after all, in case she had forgotten. But the words locked in his throat as he stood transfixed in the sitting room doorway. Staring into the entry hall at a woman who looked the same, yet different.

Was it her hair, shining a dozen glorious shades in a soft halo about her head? Or perhaps it was the dress, a burnt orange sheath that could have looked garish, but instead suffused her skin with a warm golden sheen.

What had happened to the pink gumboots and abbreviated shorts? What had happened to the Phoebe that he recognised and could at least, to a degree, predict?

In fact, Phoebe seemed to glow all over and a thought struck Max like a poisoned dart. Did she glow because of Brent? Had Max's gardener made Phoebe look this way and, if so, what the hell had he *done* to make her so? The guy was what? Nineteen? Twenty? It was so young.

Yes, and Phoebe wasn't a whole lot older. Certainly not so old that she couldn't be attracted to someone Brent's age. Max, on the other hand, was almost thirty-five. Practically in his dotage in comparison. Not that he was making comparisons. He was over the wanting Phoebe thing. No doubt his body would catch up with that decision any time now.

'Don't worry, Max, I'll be fine to care for the boys in the morning.' She slipped her foot from her sandal and reached down with one small hand to massage the instep. 'I'm not so old that I can't hold up to the occasional night out and still take care of work the next day.'

It would help if she didn't keep doing things to distract him, though.

She tipped her head to one side. 'What are you doing up, anyway? Are the boys okay? Have they been restless?'

No. It's their father who hasn't been able to settle. 'The boys are fine. Asleep.' He growled it out.

'You waited up to check on me.' As the realisation dawned on her, her face suffused with angry colour. She shoved her foot back into the sandal and glowered. 'To pry into my personal life. You had no right.'

'I'm the father of the two children in your care.' He waved a hand in her general direction. 'That gives me certain rights but, in point of fact, I wasn't waiting up for you. I just couldn't sleep, that's all. It does happen to people occasionally.'

'But once you happened to be up, you decided to cross-question me on what I'd been doing.' As she spoke, wind started to whistle through the eaves of the house in an eerie moan. 'I'll tell you. Why not, since you're so all-fired interested all of a sudden? One of Brent's sisters is training to become a hairdresser. She cut and styled my hair. Then Brent and I went shopping together. I bought this outfit from a charity shop, we swapped life stories, all that sort of thing.' Her lips curled in contempt. 'Until now, I'd had a pleasant few hours in very congenial company.'

If she meant to make him uncomfortable by this innocent-sounding rendition of her day, she failed.

'A thoroughly footloose day, in other words.' He pressed closer and felt some small measure of pleasure when she backed several steps. 'But then, that's you, isn't it? You go your own way without worrying too much about how it might affect anyone around you.'

'I permit myself to have friends. It's no crime.' She stuck her face into his until her lips were so close he swore he could sense their moist warmth.

His blood pressure hiked, and with it came anger. 'You're shiftless,' he accused. 'A rolling stone, a self-interested waif.'

'And you're an arrogant, old-fashioned, controlling bully.'

'You won't let people into your life,' he retaliated. 'You're so busy keeping everyone at bay that you're just not capable of being real.'

'That is so ridiculous.' She gave a harsh laugh. 'Point at yourself when you say that.'

'I don't feel like pointing.' Somehow he had her pushed back against the door, a hand flat against the wall on either side of her head, and the anger was real now, not whipped up for the sake of self-preservation. 'I admit I like to be in control, but at least I know who and what I am, and I face my challenges, instead of moving on all the time so none of them ever have time to catch up with me.'

'That is so wrong. You're the worst avoider of all time.' Bright splotches of colour rode high on her cheekbones. Her breath came in sharp, staccato bursts. 'You know, you've criticised me a lot in the past, Max, but you've never got this dirty about it—this personal. It's none of your concern whether I engage in life or not and, furthermore, you're the one who's not engaging. Who gave you a say in my life, anyway?'

'Not for want of trying.' Years of frustration welled to the surface and burst free. 'And, as for who gave me a say, certainly not you. I tried with you, Phoebe. God knows I tried until my guts were tied in knots and I just couldn't try any more. *You wouldn't let me in.*'

'*You hated me.*' She flung the words at him as though they would be her very salvation. 'I was a thorn in your side from the day we met. I didn't fit. You didn't want me, any more than—'

'I don't *know* why you got on my nerves. I've never understood, damn it.' Max lost it. His hands came down on her
shoulders. 'Half the time there wasn't even a reason for it,
yet you always annoyed me.'

Her anger crumpled into confusion. She whispered, 'We're
still annoying each other, aren't we? But there's more, now.'

He laughed harshly. 'Oh, there's more all right. There's
this!' He snatched her up as though a millisecond's delay
might well be fatal. Clamped his mouth across hers and
delved deep.

If she had wanted to stop him she had left it too late. Had
responded too sensually and immediately to him.

Her taste, the texture of her, he gobbled all of it like a
greedy boy suddenly in possession of the cookie jar.

And Phoebe kissed him back. Her tongue tasted of anger
and passion and for every plunge, every delving stroke he
made, she met it, parried it, returned it in full force.

All Max's pent-up emotions coalesced in the give and take
of their kiss. 'You've wanted this, needed it too.'

Her hands were locked around his neck. He couldn't say
since when. He lowered his head. Kissed a fiery trail across
her collarbone, past the spaghetti strap of her dress, and into
the indent of her shoulder. Licked that little hollow and felt
her shudder in his arms. 'Admit it, Phoebe. You need this.
You need *me*.'

Her hands were pushed up beneath his shirt, exploring
across his ribcage, on to his chest. Caressing, moulding, learn-
ing. Dear God, it felt so good. But at his words her movements stilled. Her hands flexed, once, then she pushed hard
against him. He stumbled back a step.

'You don't know me.' Her face still carried the signs of
their closeness, but her eyes flashed fire. 'You have no idea
of what I want or need.'

Before he could speak, she turned and hurried away.

CHAPTER EIGHT

A HIGH, frightened cry split the darkness. Phoebe was out of bed before the next one came. Through the corridor and into the boys' room in time to hear a third cry that combined two voices. Above their cries, wind howled in gusty wails and groans and ear-shattering shrieks.

These occasional wind storms had given Phoebe the creeps too, the first time she had experienced one out here. Nowadays, she slept straight through, but she could understand why the boys hadn't.

Jake was sitting upright in his bed, eyes like saucers, his face chalk-white. The roar of the wind built up again, then the slap of it against the house shook everything. Josh whimpered and, when the house shook, screamed too.

'What's wrong with them?' Max hit the room at a dead run, his glance going from one child to the other. 'What's happened?'

'It's the wind storm.' Phoebe snatched Jake from his bed, cuddled him close and felt his little body trembling as he clamped arms and legs around her and buried his head against her chest. 'They're terrified.'

When she turned, Max had Josh held against him in much the same manner.

He tilted his head towards the window. 'I'd forgotten what it can seem like when you're not used to it. We need to calm them down somehow.'

'Jake, Josh.' Phoebe tried to get them to make eye contact with her, but neither boy would. 'I know it's very noisy and a bit scary when the house shakes, but it's just a very big wind. We're quite safe here.'

The boys simply went on screaming.

Phoebe tried to think, but her brain was fuzzed from lack of sleep. What time would it be? Two, three in the morning? She felt as though she had only been asleep minutes before those screams had woken her.

The reason for her wakefulness reared. Max. That kiss. His determination that she should admit that she wanted him, even after she had turned down his painful marriage proposal.

Of course she wanted him. All he had to do was be somewhere in the house and she was so aware of him she couldn't think straight.

Phoebe would go further and admit that being here with Max, Jake and Josh had made her long for more than life had chosen to give her. What woman with no prospect of ever having children of her own would *not* be attracted to the possibility of an instant family?

She had tried not to let the situation get to her, but it had. And now the boys were distraught, and Phoebe felt as protective and concerned as any mother would.

Another roar of wind against the house made both boys scream. Josh started kicking into Max's legs. Jake burst into noisy sobs that fell hard upon each other.

'You're safe, Jake.' Max strode across the room to her side. Tugged her forward so he could get his hands on his second son, could hold him too. 'You and Josh are both safe. Nothing's going to happen to you here. I won't let it.'

At the deep, soothing tone of Max's voice and the caring expression etched on his face, Phoebe's already shaky stores of resistance melted further.

Max had to love these boys. How could he act this way, otherwise? Maybe, as time went on, he would let them further into his life and be a real father to them. If he could forget at times like this, then Phoebe was inclined to believe that *this* was the real Max. Not the one who wanted to keep his distance from them.

Maybe Phoebe was wrong about Max holding back emotionally for ever. Maybe she had made a mistake in rejecting his proposal. He might be able to change over time and come to care for her, as well. Her heart ached at the tantalising image of the four of them forming the kind of close-knit family that Phoebe longed for.

Fool, even to think it!

They huddled, that group of four, in the middle of the room. She and Max held a boy each and they touched them, stroked them, endeavouring to bring calm in the middle of nature's howling onslaught.

It was just a pity that this particular part of the mountainous terrain sometimes managed to bottleneck these wind storms. By morning it would all be over, with probably not even a drop of rain to go with it. But that knowledge wasn't going to help anyone just at present. Knowing she needed to resist her emotional longings wasn't helping Phoebe, either.

'I can't fight this for them.' Max's voice had a frustrated edge to it. He had to speak loudly to be heard over the wind and the boys' cries.

'My bed.' It was the only inspiration Phoebe could think of in the face of such stark terror. She stroked each small back in the hope that she had their attention, and pushed her own problems aside. 'Remember when I first came here, I told you my bed was the safest place in the house? It still is. I promise you, if you get in there you'll be safe.'

Jake nodded. Josh did nothing, but at least he wasn't fighting any more. Phoebe met Max's worried gaze. They silently took the boys into her room, but when she tried to put Jake in the bed, he clung.

'Wif you.' His breath hitched on a backed-up sob. 'Wif Phoebe.'

'Oh, baby.' Phoebe's eyes misted. She clambered into the bed with Jake wrapped around her middle like a monkey. Then she reached out to take Josh as well. The feelings swelling inside threatened to swamp her, and she felt worryingly close to emotional tears.

Sometimes Phoebe swore that her empty womb ached with the loss of the things she would never have. She may not have experienced regular periods over the years like other women, but she knew about a different kind of internal pain that was just as real and much more devastating. Being around Max and his sons had sharpened that ache.

'Come on, Josh.' She cleared her throat to get rid of the husky tremor. 'Let's snuggle up, okay?'

But Josh didn't intend to go anywhere, it seemed. He cried and buried his face in Max's bare chest.

'You don't want to get in Phoebe's bed?' Max stroked the small head. 'That's okay. We'll get in my bed, all right?'

Oh, Max. Do you know how you're torturing me right now? Please, please don't go back to being that old distant Max when this is over.

That was her fear, and as soon as she gave rein to it she acknowledged it would most likely be the reality. Max himself had made it clear that he didn't *want* to change. *She* was the one getting carried away on one or two soft words and a fanciful imagination.

'No.' Josh wailed the word and started kicking again.

'What do you want, Josh?' Phoebe kept her tone calm, although she felt anything but. Tension radiated from both boys, filling the room far more oppressively than the aggression of the roaring wind that raged beyond its walls.

Jake still trembled against her. Any sudden upset and he would start up screaming again, she knew. And Phoebe still felt emotionally raw. Examining her feelings on such a short amount of sleep was clearly not a good idea. A shame, then, that she couldn't simply turn them off at will.

'Want in the bed. All body in the bed.' Josh hiccuped his plea against Max's shoulder. 'Me and Jake and Phoebe and Daddy.'

Not a good idea. But the enticement of the four of them cuddling in the bed crept insidiously through her mind. Wrapped itself around her aching heart, doing its best to twine her into a right old tangle.

Max's gaze searched hers. Wary, reserved. But there was a plea there too. For his sons, she supposed, and that brought things back into perspective a bit. She might want to be absorbed in her own feelings and reactions right now, but she was an adult and supposedly able to contend with all that.

The boys weren't. They needed help to cope with this situation, and if they wanted that help to be in the form of all four of them in a bed, just like Goldilocks and all the bears, then Phoebe had better let them have what they wanted. Except it didn't seem much like an innocuous children's tale to her.

She shifted her gaze from Max's compelling one and threw the covers back, speaking carefully for Josh's benefit. 'Then come get in the bed. We'll all be here together.'

Josh dived in.

Max got in the bed behind him. 'Are you all right with this?'

No, of course I'm not all right with it.

She gestured with her gaze, first to Jake in her arms, then to Josh, tangled against Max's broad chest. 'They're all that matters. I'm all right with it *for as long as it proves necessary for their sakes.*'

That should make it abundantly clear that she didn't have any other ideas in mind, even if she did, which wasn't the point.

Max's jaw clenched, but he nodded. 'Believe me, if there was any other way to manage this, I'd take it.'

Ridiculously, she was inclined to feel offended. If Max found the thought of sharing a bed with her so repugnant, then why on earth had he wanted to sign up for it for the rest of his life?

Because you were here, and he had an itch he needed to scratch.

Phoebe should have kept that fact in the forefront of her mind, rather than letting herself go off on some ridiculous fancy about happy families.

Max's marriage proposal had been an anomaly. A moment of sheer insanity on his part. He didn't do long-term commitment where women were concerned, and Phoebe had best remember that fact from now on. She dropped her gaze to Jake's head. 'I'd insist that you did.'

Max shuffled Josh into a more comfortable position. 'Until they're settled, then.'

The wind blasted the house for another fifteen minutes or so, then calmed enough that the boys lost the sense of immediate threat. After a time, they fell asleep.

Phoebe didn't. It was dangerous being so close to Max this way. Despite doing her best to put a stop to her foolish dreaming, she knew this with every fibre of herself, was so attuned to the man beside her it was scary.

No matter what else happened, she planned to stay awake long enough to see him out of her bed and ensure neither child stirred enough to be disturbed by his absence. Self-preservation and duty. Those were all she needed to think about for now.

But the storm and the emotional upheaval that had preceded it earlier in the evening took their toll. She fell asleep with one small boy curled against her and another one sleeping in his father's arms just a hand span away. And she fell asleep smiling and content because, despite all her efforts not to, a part of her kept saying that this was the way it should be.

Time passed unheeded until noise infiltrated Phoebe's sleep. The TV in the sitting room. Cartoons, to be exact, and the muted morning chatter of two small boys out there who had probably already forgotten the wind storm had even happened.

As the sleep haze faded from her mind, Phoebe realised she felt happy. Incredibly so. Relaxed and happy and warm. The bed seemed to support her, surround her with heat and comfort.

She sighed and moved a hand, a tiny stroking motion that was brought up short at the realisation that what she touched was not mattress, bedcovers or pillow.

None of those breathed gently beneath her touch. None held the living warmth of skin and the teasing prickle of curling chest hair. None made her breath catch in her throat and her skin tingle with sensual delight.

Max was still in the bed with her. It was Max, not the bed, upon which her head currently rested and, for that matter, quite a lot else of her rested too. Even as her body quickened to the feel of his, she moaned inwardly.

With her eyes squinched shut, she tried to assess their exact positions. Her movements elicited a groan from Max. She attempted to wriggle away from him, but he held her fast.

In fact, they were pressed together like lovers. Max had an arm slung over her shoulders and one of her legs rested between his. It didn't get a whole lot more intimate than this, as her betraying body seemed intent on confirming more and more with each passing second.

This had to stop. What if he woke up and discovered how closely they were pressed together? She caught her breath. Laid her hand flat against Max's chest preparatory to pushing away from him. Something about his stillness alerted her before she could do so. She opened her eyes and looked up into the most sleep-heated blaze she had ever seen.

Thoughts of self-preservation and being sensible and protecting her heart as best she could dissolved in the heat of that look. Phoebe wanted, simply, to dig into it, bury herself in it, and let it take her wherever it would.

'Good morning.' The words were deep and rumbled in a

sleepy tone, yet the look in his eyes was anything but slumbrous. 'I see you decided to join me on my side of the bed.'

'I didn't.' The denial came automatically. But she had for, now that she looked, Max was right where he should have been in the bed. It was she who had moved. She who had slithered over the intervening space and pressed herself all over him like a wanton.

'You're not supposed to still be here.' She tried to push back from him, but one lazy hand rose and locked hers to his chest. 'You were supposed to leave last night after they fell asleep.' This time her tone bordered on a wail. She clamped her teeth shut and prayed to high heaven that she wouldn't give herself away any further.

She was supposed to be over all this. Over Max. Over wanting him. Over wanting him to care about her, for goodness' sake. She wasn't supposed to turn to him in her subconscious, as though he were the best thing that had ever happened to her.

'I'm well aware I was supposed to leave your bed, Phoebe.' He shrugged. 'It just happened that I fell asleep before I could carry out your wishes, that's all.' Each word he spoke rumbled beneath her hand, making her want to lean her ear against his chest and feel that vibration as intimately as she could.

She pulled her hand free and scooted to the other side of the bed in a move that was one hundred per cent self-preservation. 'Well then, you can leave now. I need to have a shower, and somebody should be watching the boys. They've obviously helped themselves to the TV. Let's just hope they haven't taken it into their heads to get breakfast as well.'

'They've been chattering away with that TV show for ages.' His gaze rested on her, dark and tempting. 'I'm sure they're fine.'

'But *I'm* not fine.' She didn't want to get out of the bed with Max's lazy eyes watching her, taking in every part of her in the early morning light. She certainly couldn't stay here with him, with that devilish look on his face, and her own senses tempting her to do all the wrong things, for all the wrong reasons.

She had a strong feeling that Max wasn't thinking in his usual controlled and orderly manner right now, either. Which meant she had to do the thinking for both of them.

It suddenly hit her, just what Max had said and what it meant. Which only proved she must be right about him not being his usual reserved self at the moment. She bunched the covers up under her chin. 'How long have you been awake?'

His lips relaxed into a feral grin. 'Long enough to experience the sensation of you snoring lightly on my chest in little puffy breaths, then slowly coming awake as your senses pushed you out of the sleep zone and into awareness of me.'

'I wasn't aware, not the way you mean, and I certainly would not have snored on you.'

'Well, at least you didn't dribble.'

Her outrage swelled and swamped her. She spluttered before she found her voice again. 'You took advantage of me. I didn't know where I was, what I was doing.'

'Afraid you were forcing your attentions on me?' He quirked an eyebrow, clearly enjoying himself. 'Worried about what you might have done, or even said, while sleep claimed you?'

It was exactly what bothered her. She could have said anything. Could have begged in her sleep, revealed her secrets and any or all of those pesky longings that she worked so hard to pretend didn't exist during waking hours. She snatched the pillow from behind her and thwacked it square into the side of his head. 'Get out of my bed right now.'

Max drew the pillow away. He was no longer smiling. He wasn't angry, but the light-heartedness had left him, replaced by something deeper, darker. 'I'll bet you wouldn't carry on like this if it was Brent in the bed with you.'

'Of course not.' As if she would get into bed with the school-age gardener! What a stupid thing for him to say. 'There's no comparison.'

'I see.' Max's eyes took on a glitter that made her catch her breath. 'No comparison, huh?'

'None at all.' Max didn't seem to be getting the point. She wished he would drop the whole silly topic and just get out of her bed and be done with it. *I need to regroup here, Max, and you're not helping me to achieve that goal.*

'Let's see if *this* convinces you otherwise.' Max's long arms reached out. He snatched her across the bed.

His mouth was on hers before she could so much as draw breath, let alone protest that there was no need for him to convince her of anything. The heat of his skin filtered through her thin nightgown, swamping her even as his tongue pressed for entry to her mouth.

She moaned and let him in. There would be time to hate herself later, she decided, without engaging any brain cells whatsoever in the decision. Yes, when her hormones weren't driving her to a response she couldn't seem to check, *then* she could worry about the wisdom of doing this.

Max's hands were everywhere. Hers were too; she just couldn't stop herself. While he cupped and stroked and shaped, she clutched, dug her nails into his broad shoulders and shuddered beneath an onslaught that was all the more powerful because she had wanted it so much against her will.

'We're going to finish this, once and for all.' Max's hands rucked her nightwear up to her thighs. The feel of his lean fingers on her legs brought a low, keening sound from her throat.

She fought for breath. For words. For a single thread of self-control. 'What do you mean?'

His answer was a growl and a hot, determined plundering of her senses that left her trembling with need, her thoughts blown away like so many wisps of smoke driven before the wind.

Things were on the brink of getting seriously out of hand when a small, high voice called from the living room.

'Daddee. I'm hungree.'

Max's body covered hers. With a hand at her breast, the other cupping her face, holding it still for his plunder, and his face etched in dark desire, he had Phoebe quivering with need for him.

She would have given him everything in that moment, would have lived to regret it for the rest of her life.

This is just lust on his part, remember? You're nothing special to him. You just happen to be here.

And, at this moment, making herself far too available to him. Panting, struggling to draw back from that most dangerous precipice, she closed her eyes and gave thanks for small boys with empty tummies.

'I'll feed them and come back.' His words were low, edged in a hunger that had nothing to do with food. 'They can watch a video or something.'

She clamped her lips into a tight line and shook her head. With a determined effort, she forced her eyes open and looked at him. 'We're not finishing this in the way you had in mind. All it would prove is that we were both capable of being as stupid as each other.'

For a moment, she thought Max's jaw might snap, so strong was the tension in it. Then he pushed away from her, rolled from the bed and stalked from the room in jerky movements, his silence transmitting his irritation.

Phoebe may have snuggled on to Max inadvertently, in her sleep, but if anyone was culpable for what had passed between them after that, it was Max. He was the one who seemed to think he had something to prove.

'And Brent's practically a child, Max,' she called after him. 'A year ago, he was still in school.'

'Do something with the boys,' he called back. 'I'm going to take a shower.' Slam.

'Well, good for you then,' Phoebe muttered. 'Martyr.' She scrambled out of the bed, ripping the sheets off it as she went. 'No way I'm getting back in there with any reminders of last night either, like the warm, wonderful scent of him.' When she realised what she had muttered, she threw the sheets into the corner with a disgusted snap of her wrist. She had to get out of here.

Tossing herself into the first clothes that came to hand, she hurried out to the boys. Once she had them dressed and tidied, she paused in the hallway.

'I'm taking the boys to breakfast at Yolanda's,' she shouted in the general direction of the bathroom. Frankly, she didn't care whether Max understood her or not.

A muffled response came through the door. It could have been *Yes* or *No*, or *Where the heck is that?* Whatever it was, she ignored it and bundled the boys outside.

Running away? That depended on how you looked at the matter. It was, after all, a nanny's prerogative to treat her charges to breakfast out occasionally. Phoebe stepped down on the accelerator of the small car, glanced in her rear-view mirror at the house and, seeing no signs of movement, let out a sigh of relief.

'Mind if I join you?' Max had just spent twenty minutes under a cold shower and another five dripping all over the carpet while he took a phone call he didn't want to know about. He was not a happy camper, and Phoebe taking his sons off into the wild blue yonder for breakfast had only added to his annoyance.

'By all means.' She waved a nonchalant arm while her other hand remained curled around a cappuccino.

When she slid further along the bench seating, Max followed her in, deliberately sprawling his thighs until she was crowded into the corner. The small measure of satisfaction gained from this childish behaviour did nothing to ease his irritation.

Phoebe shot him a dagger look, concealed behind a smiling display of teeth, and offered to order him some breakfast.

'No, thank you. *I* ate at the house.' He cast a thunderous glance at his sons, then realised it would scare them and quickly smoothed it into an inquiring glance. 'Enjoying the waffles, boys?'

'Yes, Daddy.'

'They's good, Daddy.'

'That's great.' This topic dealt with, and his sons immersed to their noses again in sticky, syrupy waffles, Max drummed his fingers on the table and tried not to watch while Phoebe took a slow, sensuous draught of her coffee.

It was impossible to ignore her, when simply being close made him want to grab her, ravish her. Max's tension spiked higher. Those moments in her bed this morning had turned him inside out. Her rejection had cost him more than a dose of frustration.

He had felt offended, damn it, and didn't really even understand his own reaction. This irrationality and the feeling of not wanting to be away from her right now were driving him insane. 'I have to go to Adelaide.'

She set the cup down. A film of froth clung to her upper lip, and she licked it away in an efficient motion that shouldn't have made his gut clench, nor his groin ache with that same want he had tried to freeze out of existence so recently.

'I don't think I understand.' She produced a wet wipe from a bag beneath the table, swiped both his sons with it so quickly they didn't get time to protest, and suggested they go play in Yolanda's backyard. 'I'll come and get you in a moment, okay?'

Given that there were toys aplenty out there and those toys

could be seen through the plate-glass doors and windows, Jake and Josh quickly nodded and made their escape.

'I had a call from Maryellen's solicitors. It'll only take a couple of days, three at the most, but there are things I have to settle.'

'Oh. I see.' She dropped her gaze and focused on disposing of the grubby cloth before she finally faced him again. 'When?'

'Now. I'm packed. It's all in the car.' And he, who always did his duty, would have delegated this to someone else in a heartbeat if anyone else could have handled it.

'I'll do my best with the boys while you're gone.'

'I don't want—' He broke off, uncertain just what it was that he did want.

'It's all right. I understand.' She turned her face aside. 'This is something you have to do.'

She stood, collected the boys and enticed them out of the building with the promise of a long play in the sandpit when they got home.

When they all stood outside on the footpath beside Max's car, she addressed the boys. 'Your dad has to go away for just a little while. Three sleeps, maybe. Give him a kiss and say goodbye, and then we're going to go back to the house, okay?'

She pushed both boys forward with a gentle hand to their shoulders. Max leaned down and received two generously given sloppy kisses. He didn't want to leave Jake and Josh, either. Not now. And not when he returned to work either, he realised. But walking away of his own accord had to be better than having them beg for him to do so later. Didn't it?

He rolled his shoulders and shoved his hands into his pockets. 'I'll phone.'

'I'll understand if you don't.'

What did she mean by that? Don't bother calling? That was what it sounded like to him. By the time he got into his car,

Phoebe had the boys inside her smaller one and was strapping them in, securing them.

Unwilling to show his frustration with the situation, Max gave a meaningless wave without making eye contact and drove away.

CHAPTER NINE

PHOEBE hadn't been so fed up since, well, since she couldn't remember when. She had been through a difficult time since her arrival at Mountain Gem, darn it all, and did anyone care?

No. She had to deal with her issues by herself, as usual, and while she was dealing with them Max kept heaping more hassles on to her. Like making her want to make love with him. Marry him. Play families with him. If he didn't have his boys, Phoebe wouldn't care about them, would she? If she hadn't come here to help Max out, she wouldn't have ended up in bed with him, would she?

In her current state of mind, the argument made perfect sense. Just thinking about it all again made her want to breathe fire, and with very good reason. If ever there was a man undeserving of one millisecond of her consideration, it was Max Saunders.

He had gone off to attend to Maryellen's estate. And Phoebe had felt sorry for him, because he had looked so torn. So stirred up. As if he didn't want to have to leave her and the boys right now.

Even with her own conflicting feelings, it had been enough to make Phoebe want to turn around and tell him to just stay. Or that she and the boys would go with him. Anything for them all to be together. What a fool she had been to think along those lines, and thank God she hadn't actually made love to Max that morning in her bed.

Which brought her to the question—why be so relieved about that now? Because of Felicity Danvers, that was why. She realised her jaw was locked again and tried to work it loose.

The day after Max had left, the woman had turned up on the doorstep with her pencil-thin laptop computer and her business suit and her matching luggage—all seven pieces of it—and, upon being told Max wasn't there, had replied, 'That's all right. I've been working at a frantic pace. A couple of days' rest will ensure I'm at my best before Max returns. Really, the timing couldn't have been better.'

She had released her taxi—'I lost my driver's licence speeding on the Great Ocean Road, you know'—and stalked confidently into the house.

That might have been half tolerable—well, not really, but Phoebe might have lived with it, but it hadn't stopped there. Oh, no.

To Phoebe's admirably controlled query as to the purpose of her visit, Felicity had replied, 'I'm here to make Max's day, darling. A business deal he simply won't be able to say no to and, well…' she had paused coyly '…some other things he'll be equally unwilling to resist. Now, get me a cup of tea, would you, and stop pestering me with questions. I really don't have time to instruct the help.'

Phoebe had restrained herself from hitting the other woman over the head with a conveniently placed lampshade nearby, but it had been a close-run thing for a minute.

To Phoebe's flat comment that she was the nanny, not the help, Felicity had raised a carefully plucked eyebrow and informed her there was no difference, before suggesting she be a good girl, get the tea and bring in the luggage too, so that Felicity would be able to give Max a nice report about her when he got back.

Needless to say, the luggage had sat there until Felicity collected it herself. Phoebe had made the tea, but only because she was basically a very nice human being.

The woman's presence in the house reminded Phoebe of Max's true nature. How could it not? Felicity was what Max was about. Felicity and all the other women who were the same type. And the woman may not have had time to *instruct* the help, but she appeared to have time to *grill* it. She proceeded to do so, completely disregarding the fact that she had offended Phoebe when she'd arrived, and had done nothing to mitigate that situation since.

Felicity wanted to hear all about Max, his lifestyle and his spending habits. She hadn't been impressed when Phoebe explained the presence of Max's sons. Apparently that was one piece of information that hadn't managed to reach Felicity's interested ears already.

But Felicity clearly wasn't going to let their presence get in her way. Hers may have been an unscheduled visit, but she was clearly here to get her claws into Max and was utterly confident she could do so.

Phoebe gritted her teeth and tried to stay sane. Hence her presence *outside* the house with the boys, while Felicity held court on her own within. If the woman didn't have a business purpose for being here as well, Phoebe would have forced her out of the house. As it was, she didn't feel she could.

Phoebe stroked a deceptively light hand over the newly installed veranda lattice and sucked in a breath of humid air. The day was hot, oppressive. Much like the atmosphere inside the house, really.

'Try pressing the red button, Josh.' She pointed to the button in question and watched as Josh pressed it and crowed his delight when the battery-operated train began to move in the opposite direction on its tracks. 'That's the way.'

Jake sat further along the veranda, surrounded by rubber toys, immersed in his own game of make-believe. Phoebe wished she could *make-believe* the woman inside Max's house to kingdom come.

The worst part about it was that Felicity, despite the way she grated on Phoebe, was everything Phoebe wasn't. A smart, stunning, upmarket career woman who clearly knew exactly where she was headed and how she planned to get there. Phoebe felt dowdy and stupid in comparison.

'You out there.' The grating voice wafted out on to the veranda. 'I thought I told you that I wanted a pot of tea made.'

'She must have heard me thinking about her,' Phoebe muttered. She clenched her teeth to stop herself from shouting back something she shouldn't and, at the same time, noticed a vehicle approaching along the lane.

Max. Home at last. Suddenly every insinuation that Felicity Danvers had slung at Phoebe over the past two days rose up in a choking wave. To listen to Felicity tell it, she and Max would be tearing each other's clothes off the moment he stepped out of his car and, of course, later they would discuss that little business arrangement too. As if it was a total afterthought.

Max was a worm, Phoebe decided, while visions of him and Felicity together danced through her head. A snake. *A toad on a worm on a snake.*

He had asked Phoebe to marry him, but he hadn't meant it. He must have been so relieved when she had turned him down! All Max had ever wanted was a willing body. And Phoebe had let herself care. The willing body was waiting inside and Phoebe still cared, despite herself. It was a good thing she was too angry to dwell on the fact. She grimaced and waited for Max to pull to a stop nearby.

'Your father is home,' she informed the boys once he was safely parked.

They whooped and ran down the steps, probably relieved to see someone other than Felicity, given her less than sweet disposition. Phoebe followed more slowly, determined to do the nanny thing, the professional thing, if it killed her. No way would she allow Max to know how she hated the idea of him and Felicity together, so she guessed she didn't have much choice but to act this out the best way she could.

Her attitude worked just fine until Max turned from getting

his bags out of the back, saw her and broke into a smile so
sweet and so sensual that, for a moment, Phoebe forgot everything and just stared, all the longing she had thought was
killed off rising to the surface again.

Why did he have to be this way? Why couldn't he stay in
character, instead of giving her these intermittent peeks at
something that could be so much better, if only he really
meant it?

*It's only your imagination that he's happy to see you. Most
likely, Max smiled because he was hoping you'd be there to
help carry his bags inside.*

*Yeah, just call me Packhorse. Felicity seems to think it fits
well enough.*

The boys laughed and danced around, but Max just stood,
looking at Phoebe, desiring her and doing nothing to try to
hide the fact that he did.

The snake. The toad. The worm. How could he?

He stepped towards her. 'Phoebe, I've missed—'

'You have a visitor.' The words were so gravelly with anger that Phoebe hardly recognised her own voice. She knew
her face must have shown every bit of contempt she felt, all
the more vehement for the self-disgust that went with it.

How could she have reacted to Max for even one second,
when she knew how much of a swine he was? Max Saunders
couldn't be faithful if his life depended on it. Anything in a
skirt would no doubt do, and frequently did, it seemed.

'What are you talking about?' Max's expression was all
puzzlement.

'You can't guess?' Phoebe swung around and started
climbing the veranda steps. 'Let me give you a hint. Long
legs? Daddy owns a lot of jewellery stores?'

'Felicity Danvers.' Max clasped her arm to stop her from
moving and swung her round to face him. 'Are you saying
Felicity is here?'

'For the past two very long days.' She shrugged her arm

free and kept walking. 'I realise it's probably a lot to ask, but try to keep yourself from throwing her down on the carpet until you've got her some place private, will you? There are impressionable children in the house.'

And a very angry nanny, besides.

Max shot her a thunderous glare. 'What the hell are you talking about?'

'It was a simple request, Max. I'm sure that if you think about it you'll work it out.'

While Max's jaw worked Phoebe called to the boys, who'd become distracted by their toys, and stomped into the house, falsely cheerful, promising a bubble bath and their favourite dinner since they had been so good all day.

'Your father will read you a story tonight.' She gave Max a venomous glance as he followed her in. 'I'm sure he'll be able to spare that much time from his guest, for the sake of his darling sons.'

Before Max could argue, or tell her she had overstepped the bounds yet again, the *guest* spoke.

'Max, dearest.' Felicity, all stylised blonde hair and tanned, slender legs, rose from her indolent position on the living room couch and flung herself against Max's chest.

Don't worry, Phoebe counselled herself. *She'll get sofa spread sooner or later. She won't be smiling quite so confidently when she has to prise her butt out of the lounge cushions with a crowbar.*

Phoebe kept walking, wishing she hadn't been exposed to even that much of the Max and Felicity Reunion Show. Wishing she could kick the other woman in the shins and then kick Max as well, just to even the score.

The last thing she saw, as she snapped the bathroom door shut behind her and the boys, was Max's hands coming up to clasp Felicity's arms. No doubt in another second the pair would be sucking each other's lips off, and that was a sight that Phoebe just couldn't stand to see.

She turned the bath taps on full blast and told herself she didn't care. Not one single iota. If Felicity wanted to indulge in a fling with Max, good for her. Big whoop. Phoebe didn't need any of this, anyway. She was fine on her own. Maybe. Perhaps. In her dreams.

And if she wanted to run away as far and as fast as she could she quickly stifled the urge. She had a job to do, and she would do it, no matter how tough. Otherwise, it would look as if she cared what Max did, wouldn't it? Not an impression she had any intention of giving!

'What are you doing here, Felicity?' Max detached the clinging fingers and held her away from him, trying to keep his frustration under control.

None of this was going to plan. Phoebe was angry. He hadn't even had the time to greet his boys before she'd whisked them away from him, and he had wanted to greet them, damn it, despite that being contrary to what he believed he *should* do.

'I guess you could say I'm an emissary,' Felicity purred. She lifted a finger to stroke inside the collar of Max's shirt. Her eyes were full of avarice, and a hard-edged, selfish kind of lust that Max thoroughly disliked.

Max pulled back. 'An emissary for what?'

Felicity laughed and threw her head back, exposing the long line of her throat. 'Why for my father's business, of course,' she declared. 'If our negotiations go well over the next couple of days, I should be able to make you a very pleasant offer.'

Max didn't want to negotiate for a couple of days. Not even for a couple of hours. This was not the homecoming he had hoped for although, given Phoebe's irrational anger when he'd arrived, he wondered if he was mad to have missed being here. The angry virago who'd just shut herself in the bathroom with his sons wasn't exactly what he had expected to see.

Maybe he'd been crazy to rush home on that gut feeling that he needed to be where she was.

When he thought about it that way, it *was* mad. Hell, he didn't know. He just felt unsettled. As though there was unfinished business between them.

What unfinished business would that be? The bit about getting married? She's already made her thoughts on that subject quite clear.

Equally clear was Phoebe's unwillingness to pursue intimacy with him under any other guise. So what did the woman want? Ten quarts of blood, sole ownership of his business and a sizeable chunk out of his hide? And that was just for starters. But no, now that he thought about it, that was more like a description of what Felicity wanted out of him.

'Max, darling, were you listening?' Felicity pouted and would have wrapped her arms around him again if he hadn't swiftly turned aside.

'Yes, I listened.' He just didn't want her here, that was all. 'You're talking about your company's overseas business interests, I assume.'

'That's right.' She gave a feline smile. 'There's so much I have to offer you, if the climate is right for an agreement.'

'So make me the offer. We'll sort it out, and you can go.' He was appalled that she had simply turned up here and made herself at home in the first place. The sheer audacity of it left him all but speechless.

Phoebe had said nothing of Felicity's presence on the two occasions that Max had phoned. She had been distant enough that he had decided not to ring again after the second time, preferring to talk to her in person when he got home. Perhaps he should have asked what the problem was. At least he would have been forearmed.

As Felicity smiled at him again—a sultry woman's smile that declared as clearly as words that she thought she could bend him to her will with patent ease—Max's temper snapped. He really didn't have time for her machinations right now. 'The deal. Spit it out, and let's stop wasting time.'

For a moment, anger turned Felicity's features into an ugly mask. Then she shook her head and gave a smile of tolerant disapproval. 'All in good time, Max. I rushed here directly from a very hectic two weeks of globe-trotting. I'm still working on the details of the agreement our company can put to you, getting my figures together. I'm afraid if you want to talk business, you're going to have to put up with me a little longer first.'

Max weighed his choices. Throw her out and lose the deal, or let her stay and make sure he gained it. How annoying could she be for another twenty-four hours? And it wasn't his fault that Phoebe was in a snit. He hadn't invited Felicity here, after all. Even so, he had to bite back an expletive. 'Your father—'

'Off at one of his retreats,' Felicity put in quickly. 'He's not even taking emergency calls, not that it makes any difference to our little situation. I know you'll be more than glad to…interact with me.'

Max's anger simmered in a hot wave beneath his skin. 'I'm always willing to *discuss business* with you.'

If Felicity thought he was interested in anything else, she could go sing for it. Max turned, about to brush past her and get some distance. Noise from behind him heralded the emergence of Phoebe and his sons from the bathroom, and he paused.

Felicity seemed to take that as some kind of signal to push her body against his. While Max gripped her arms to push her away from him, his boys edged their way around them and slipped into their room.

Phoebe cast Max a disgusted glare and hustled past, practically crawling along the wall herself to avoid getting close to him.

'Phoebe,' Max rasped in a warning tone, 'could you wait a moment, please? I'd like to talk to you about the boys—'

'They missed you, I can't imagine why.' Phoebe stuck her nose in the air and glared at him, as though daring him to react. 'But they've been fine. I've looked after them properly, despite the disruptions around the household just lately.'

Until then, Max had been willing to explain that despite Felicity's blatant interest in him, he wasn't interested in her. That he hadn't invited this visit. Now he wondered why he would bother.

Phoebe was jumping to conclusions all over the place, as usual. Why should he care, anyway? She had made it clear she wanted nothing to do with him so, really, what happened between him and Felicity was none of Phoebe's business. 'Fine, then. I'm glad the boys have been okay.'

He still intended to get rid of Felicity Danvers in short order, though. That intention proved tougher than Max thought it would be.

For starters, Felicity slept in so late the next day that it was after lunch before he even got a chance to speak to her. When he requested a conference she agreed readily enough, then spent the next hour and a half closeted in his study with him, speaking about everything but business.

A great portion of her conversation revolved around her desire to further herself and take a good man along with her. Max felt as if he was butting heads with a particularly resistant brick wall, and silently gave thanks when Felicity declared she needed to spend just a little more time on her proposal, then she would get right to it, she promised.

She proceeded to spend the afternoon alternating between conversing on her cellphone all over the house as though nobody else were present and somehow managing to set everybody's backs up, just by being there. Felicity had a way of irritating the life out of people, and it soon became clear Max wasn't the only one suffering the consequences of that particular personality trait of hers. Maybe Phoebe's anger was more justified than Max had first thought.

That charitable opinion didn't last long. Phoebe wasn't even prepared to give Max the time of day. If he entered the same room that Phoebe was in, she would glare at him, ask how he and Felicity were doing in a tone that insinuated she hoped they choked on each other, and rush the boys off elsewhere.

He wasn't doing anything with Felicity, and it annoyed Max that Phoebe thought so poorly of him as to believe otherwise. He decided to shut himself in his study while Felicity played whatever games she thought she was playing. Maybe, if he denied her access to him, she would realise she was wasting her time and hand over the business proposal.

But the sounds of unhappy children soon drew Max out into the sitting room again. He entered the room to discover both boys grizzling and sporting red noses.

They hadn't cried for so long that Max had forgotten how tense it made him. Phoebe had been attempting to play a simple card game with them, he gathered, and Felicity was sitting in state on the sofa, looking down her nose at the whole scene. Why didn't she go elsewhere, if it bugged her so much? Or finish her business and leave the house altogether. That would be even better.

Max moved to Phoebe's side and spoke quietly. 'What's the problem?'

'They've got head colds.' Phoebe scowled at him, but her face softened when it turned to his sons.

'Do you want me to drive you all to the doctor's?' He didn't know how to manage childhood illnesses at this age. How threatening was a cold for a four-year-old?

'Much as I'd like a shortcut to the problem, there wouldn't be any point.' For the first time in days, Phoebe's tone was weary, rather than openly hostile. 'The doctor would just tell us the colds will be gone in a day or two and suggest an over-the-counter medicine, which I already have. I noticed the medicine supplies were a bit sparse, and stocked up on anything I thought we might need last time I picked up groceries.'

She was always thinking of things Max didn't. Was so much better at caring for his boys than he would ever be. But Max wanted to try. 'I'll help you take care of them, then.'

Phoebe nodded, accepting that, if nothing else. For a long moment, Max's gaze was tender as he watched her. She wasn't looking at him, and he let his eyes rove over her at will until they came to rest on the top of her wild, ridiculous hair. He had missed that hair. Had missed all of her. Very much. Too much to remain at odds with her over a stupid misunderstanding.

He shouldn't have let her believe there was something going on between him and Felicity. Max decided that he would explain matters. Would make her see that all he cared about where Felicity was concerned was business.

With a bit of luck and manoeuvring on his part, perhaps he could get things settled with Felicity, get rid of her and get things back to normal here by the end of the day. But first he had to help with the boys and find a moment to speak with Phoebe alone, in order to explain.

Neither goal occurred that day, though, and after Max spent an exhausting night taking care of Jake while Phoebe tended to Josh in her own room, Max wondered if things would ever be the same again.

The one thing he could do, Felicity made impossible the next day by stalling again when he asked to finalise their business. Max bit down on the desire to tell her just what a selfish, thoughtless cow she was and turned his attention once more to his sons.

It was obviously some sort of waiting game Felicity was playing. Max just didn't see what she thought she would achieve by it. He had noticed her casting dagger glances at Phoebe more than once recently, though.

Max did his best to hold on to his temper, but when one of the boys started grizzling for the hundredth time that morning and the other immediately joined in, words poured out of his mouth without any conscious thought on his part. 'Are you sure they wouldn't be allowed at daycare?' His gaze sought Phoebe's across the room. 'They *were* supposed to start today.'

At Max's hounded tone, Phoebe bristled. She was tired. She had put up with Felicity ogling Max, stroking his arm and generally making it clear that, despite his acting in an utterly circumspect manner towards her in Phoebe's presence, he was smitten with Felicity. Phoebe knew what they got up to behind that closed study door.

And now this! Max's question wasn't in the least considerate of the boys' needs.

'I want to go to daycare.' This snuffled demand came from Josh as Phoebe mopped his nose again. 'I'm sick of this house!' In accompaniment to this statement, he stamped his foot.

'I know you're looking forward to daycare, Josh.' Phoebe quickly hugged him and gave Max a slit-eyed glower. 'But children aren't allowed to go to daycare when they have colds, in case they pass them on to everyone else. Remember I explained that earlier?'

A pity that Max hadn't listened at the time.

Josh's bottom lip drooped and quivered. 'Outside, then, to play.'

'It's raining.' Despite her best efforts, an edge of desperation slipped into Phoebe's tone. It had been raining since they had got up that morning, which wasn't helping much. 'Remember, I explained we can't go out there until the rain stops? Getting wet when you feel sick would make you worse.'

'The poor little darlings. Isn't there anything you can do to make them more comfortable?' Felicity asked the question in honeyed tones from her seat on the couch.

'I'm doing all I can,' Phoebe gritted, and resisted the urge to push Jake and his green nose over to Felicity with an invitation for her to take a turn at tissue-wielding duty if she was so keen to be *helpful*.

The boys didn't deserve to suffer as a result of Phoebe's anger, though, which was the only thing that stopped her.

What did Max see in Felicity?

Love conquers all.

It was the first thought to pop into Phoebe's head, but it did not apply to Max very much. 'More like *lust makes men stupid.*'

'I beg your pardon?' Felicity's perfect eyebrows rose in matched arches.

'Nothing.' Phoebe turned from her, wondering what she could do to keep the boys happy when the poor things felt so out of sorts.

'What about taking them out to a movie?' Felicity said. 'Or shopping, or something?'

'Or perhaps they could be allowed to rest easy in their own home while they're trying to recover their good health.' Phoebe's patience had run out. She caught each boy by one hand, squeezed gently, and started to shepherd them from the room. 'Let's go see what we can find to do in your bedroom, hmm? Maybe a nice story or something.'

As she walked away she heard Max heading for his study, then the click of his door as it closed, and wondered how Felicity would like being deserted again. Oh, well. It wasn't her problem.

The boys wanted *Saggy Baggy Elephant* and, naturally, Phoebe had left the book in the living room. She reluctantly left the boys and returned to retrieve the book. It was just her luck that she had left it in there with Her Buttship.

'What are *you* doing here?' Felicity's snarled question shocked Phoebe.

'Getting a book,' Phoebe said. 'Caring for Max's sons does

occasionally require that I move about from room to room throughout the house.' She strode across to the big toy hamper in the corner, hoping to find the book quickly and get away again.

'You think you're so wonderful, don't you,' Felicity sneered, 'pretending to care for those two horrors.'

What was this woman's problem? Phoebe swung around, her temper flaring. Before she had even realised her own intention, she stood facing the couch, her back to the hallway behind her, her gaze fixed disparagingly on Felicity's face. 'I don't know what's gotten your goat all of a sudden, but my relationship with Jake and Josh is no business of yours.'

How dared this woman criticise Phoebe's charges? How dared she? Phoebe's reaction was pure misplaced parenthood. She knew it, she even acknowledged the futility of it, but she couldn't make it go away. She was as hooked on Jake and Josh as it was possible to be and, if she was honest, caring about the boys was only the tip of the iceberg, in terms of her problems.

So when I leave here, I'll advertise for a mail-order family. There's bound to be a husband and kids out there just waiting for someone like me to come into their lives.

The sarcastic thought was stupid, but at least it distracted her for a second.

'Don't think you'll be here to watch over them for long.' Felicity flicked her hair over her shoulder in a practised move that made Phoebe want to scratch her eyes out. 'Not once I've taken control of matters around the place.'

'I'll be here as long as Max and I agree I will,' Phoebe tossed back, 'and I'm afraid if you think Max will give you any kind of permanent relationship, Felicity, you're fooling yourself. He doesn't do commitment and permanency. Surely you realise that?'

Until this very moment Phoebe had believed this, but now doubt crept in. Had Felicity and Max come to some sort of agreement? Had Max decided to make Felicity a permanent part of his life somehow?

'Actually, you're the fool.' Felicity sat up, swung both feet to the floor and stood to face Phoebe, thin hands on elegant, feline hips. Not a sign of a spreading butt about her, for all that she hadn't expended a calorie worth of energy in the past three days. 'You're in love with Max, and he just thinks you're an embarrassment.'

Max had talked about her? Had said things to this woman, disparaging her? Not that she *did* love Max, Phoebe assured herself. She couldn't possibly, and if Max thought she did— well, then, he was deluded.

This silent assurance did nothing to tame the mortification that threatened to engulf her. She heard shuffling sounds nearby, but was too distraught to investigate. 'You don't know anything about me or my feelings.'

'No?' Felicity looked down her cosmetically straightened nose as though inspecting a particularly ugly bug. 'You're as transparent as glass, with your jealous stares and your glaringly obvious efforts to impress him through his brats.'

'They're not brats. How dare you call them that? The boys are worth every second of time I put into them,' Phoebe hissed, 'purely for their own sakes. Caring for them is the most rewarding thing I've done in my life to date, and I certainly won't be giving it up at your say so.'

The vehemency of her own words took her breath away. Phoebe accepted it then. That she had fallen for Josh and Jake, and there would never be any going back. If—no, *when*—she left here, leaving them would be like parting with two really important parts of herself.

She had come into this situation joking with herself about empty womb syndrome. She wasn't laughing now. Phoebe wanted the opportunity to mother these boys and, just as any woman must feel about a child she bore in her own body, Phoebe knew that nothing else would do.

For the first time, she didn't feel empty because of what her body couldn't do for her. Instead, she felt the yawning chasm of losing the boys. And Max. But she didn't want to think about that.

'You won't get a choice.' Felicity pointed one manicured finger at her. 'It only needs me to get Max eating out of my hand, and he'll do whatever I want him to.'

Phoebe should have walked away, should simply have turned her back and removed herself from the room, but she couldn't let it go. Had to punish herself by facing up to all of it, even though the thought of them together made her want to scream, throw things and lick her wounds, all at once. 'Just what will he be doing, once you've got him under your thumb?'

'Why, sending *you* away for starters, and the brats right along with you.' Felicity's expression was all self-assurance. 'There are boarding establishments for unwanted children. In time I'm sure I'll be able to convince him to get rid of them altogether. Nobody wants a bastard child, after all, let alone two of them.'

Even though Felicity couldn't have known it, the conversation had skated uncomfortably close to Phoebe's own history too. She sucked in a breath while she tried to regain her equilibrium.

'Not want to go 'way.'

'*Why*, Daddy?'

Phoebe turned in horror. Two small boys were on the point of tears in the corridor. Max stood right behind them, his study door yawning open in the background. His hands came down briefly on both small sets of shoulders. 'Go and wait in your room.'

As the boys moved to obey him, he turned to Phoebe, teeth clenched, anger etched deeply in the lines of his face.

'Tend my sons, please.' The request was softly spoken, but his expression was flint-hard, ice-cold.

Before Phoebe could do more than nod, Max stepped into the room, caught Felicity up in a sort of bear hug, and strode outside with her. A moment later a car door slammed, then another. The garage door rattled up and then Max's four-wheel drive could be heard roaring along the lane, heading away from the house.

Well, that made it pretty clear just what mattered most to Max. He obviously wanted Felicity to himself, somewhere private where they could slake their mutual lust without worrying about possible interruptions. No doubt he would come back to the house later and berate Phoebe for upsetting his girlfriend.

Phoebe's shoulders slumped and tears stung behind her eyelids. She had never seen such raw volatility on Max's face, and it was all because of Felicity. All *for* Felicity.

CHAPTER TEN

ANGER had a way of burning away other feelings, or at least concealing them behind its roaring blaze. And so it was that by the time Phoebe heard Max's four-wheel drive come back into the garage late that evening she was angry beyond anything she had felt before and not about to wait a moment longer to share that anger.

The boys were sound asleep in their beds, zonked out on cold medicine and resting on reassurances about their future that Phoebe was determined to uphold. Which was just what she intended to do now. Frankly, she didn't give a blue damn if Max had brought Felicity back with him and was about to establish her in his bed and his life this very moment.

Phoebe and Max were going to have a talk. Alone. Right now. This was about Jake and Josh, and Max's responsibility to them. Enough of Max's prevaricating and running scared and refusing to commit to them for whatever the heck reasons, she didn't know.

Phoebe would see that Max did the right thing by his sons as of now. He would keep them with him and care for them properly, or she would…she would *take them from him herself*, and just see if he could stop her.

She was well aware that her thoughts were ludicrous, that she would never do any such thing, but they maintained her anger nicely. Riding on that anger, Phoebe stalked to the garage in long, floor-eating strides, her arms pumping, head thrown back, chin thrust out.

When she stepped inside the garage she slammed the house door shut behind her—a bit stupid, considering the place went instantly into pitch darkness—but she blundered forward in

125

the general direction of the driver's side of the four-wheel drive anyway, determined to get started on Max before he had a chance even to draw a breath.

The car door opened and closed, giving her a bit of light for a minute. Enough to see Max standing facing her.

That was enough. 'You're not taking them away.' Her voice had a shrill edge. She tried to adjust it, but didn't lose any of the aggression. 'Not anywhere, do you hear me? I don't care if Felicity's Godzilla in bed, those boys stay with their father, and get their father's care and attention.'

She kept moving in what she hoped was roughly the right direction. 'You owe them that much, Max. You know you do. Oomph!'

A hard chest impacted against her softer curves. Strong arms went around her, clamping her still when she would have automatically struggled free.

'I think you'd better take a breath,' Max suggested and, drat it, there was laughter in his voice. 'You seem to have got yourself in a bit of a knot.'

A bit of a knot? Phoebe struck out in the darkness, although he caught her balled fist before it could make any impact on him.

She then proceeded to wriggle and struggle as he half marched, half carried her across the double garage to the light switch, which happened to be located near the bonnet of the small car she used for ferrying the boys around. It seemed imperative to get clear of him but, so far, she was having no success.

Glaring light flooded the room when Max hit the switch, revealing the intimacy of his hold on her and the intent expression in his gaze as he looked down at her.

Phoebe sucked in a harsh breath and let fly again. 'You can't let the boys go to a boarding school or worse. Don't you realise how cruel that would be, for you to abandon them that way when they've already lost so much?'

'You're being silly.' He gave her shoulders one short, decisive shake. 'If you'll just stop rattling on long enough to listen to me—'

'It's not silly to care about your sons, Max.' She tried to thump him again, and again he restrained her. The resulting struggle found them lodged against the bonnet of the car, both of them panting hard.

'That's not what I meant.' Max's voice had dipped several notches but she was too incensed to take notice, let alone think about the implications. 'You're letting your own experiences colour your reaction.'

'Maybe I am.' She tossed her head back and glared up at him. 'If that's the case, I've got good reason to. Your boys don't deserve the kind of childhood I had, Max. Never feeling loved, always wondering what they must have done wrong to land them where they were. You can't do that to them. It's bad enough that you're holding back. If you bring Felicity into the equation, and ship them off as she wants, they'll have nothing. Nothing!'

His gaze softened. 'Phoebe—'

'Where is the woman, anyway?' She threw all her anger and disapproval into the question, because no way would she stand there and let Max pity her for her own past. Anything would be better than that, and her body was starting to react to him too. Something she *did not* want him to notice. She peered towards the four-wheel drive, but it was empty.

'Felicity's not here. I thought that would have been obvious.' The words rumbled in Max's chest, a fact Phoebe noted because he had both her hands pressed against him where she couldn't move them.

In fact, their whole bodies were pressed together more intimately than Phoebe wanted to think about, and a certain heat was beginning to rise despite her determination to tamp it down. That Max's body was reacting to hers too only incensed her more.

How dared he want her, even on that basic level, when he had just crawled out of Felicity's arms? 'Let me go.'

'In a minute. You're not trustworthy just at present.'

'That's a laugh.' She tried to squirm around so she could kick at him with her feet, but he was having none of it, holding her clamped firmly in place. 'If anyone has proved themselves to be less than trustworthy, it's you.'

Max swore succinctly and his hold tightened even further. 'Stop wriggling, or I will not be responsible for the consequences.'

Phoebe thought she really loathed him in that moment, and her words reflected the extent of her loss of self-control. 'Like a lot of men, you're not capable of thinking with anything situated above navel level, as you're proving right now, you, you…you…*man*.'

A flush rose on Max's cheekbones. 'What happened when I explained the exact nature of my relationship with Felicity to you?' he demanded. 'Right back when I first arrived home and discovered her here?'

'You *never* explained.' Phoebe wanted to stamp her feet, wail and moan and generally make a complete idiot of herself. What was happening already was bad enough. She held very still, willing the rest to stay inside her. 'You never told me a dratted thing about your relationship with her.'

'Exactly.' Aggravation infused Max's words. 'I didn't tell you anything, because you'd already made up your mind without even consulting me. As far as you were concerned, I was tried and convicted already. I didn't stand a chance.'

'You can't deny there was something—'

'That's right. There *was*.' His hands tightened on her shoulders as he looked directly into her eyes. 'I'm no saint, Phoebe. I've had women in my life. Felicity was one of them, for a very short time. I took her out. That was all. It was over before she came here, and it's still over. It'll always be over. I can't even think what I saw in her any more.'

'There was going to be a business merger.' The words wobbled from Phoebe uncertainly. 'I'm sure she said—'

'I'm sure she said a lot of things.' Max shook his head. 'I'll take their international business, if it's still on offer now that I've thrown her off the place.' He shrugged. 'If it's not, too bad. She went too far when she upset my sons.' He lowered his voice. 'And you.'

The leap of her heart was beyond Phoebe's control. She lowered her gaze, praying that Max hadn't seen the evidence of it in her eyes. 'But…her things are still here.'

His hands caressed her shoulders, shaping them in circular motions that brought her senses slowly, devastatingly to white-hot life. 'Brent can take her belongings to a courier service tomorrow and get them sent on. I really don't care.'

'She—'

Max placed a finger over her lips. 'She had an agenda. I never shared it. I was willing to tolerate her presence here in order to hear her business offering. It turns out waiting for that was a mistake.'

'I thought you wanted her close by. I thought you were attracted to her. That when you went into the study those times, you and she were—'

'We weren't.' His stormy gaze chastised her for ever thinking it.

Phoebe's hands had found their way to his chest and her body had relaxed, melting into his hold as though it, at least, knew where it belonged and what it wanted.

'Felicity wasn't very nice.' It was an understatement, but Phoebe couldn't seem to find the heated anger that had carried her through the rest of the day. She thought she should step back from Max too, get free of his hold that was so much more than a simple physical clasp.

But she didn't move. Couldn't make herself give up the thing that felt so good, so right.

'I could never send Jake and Josh away, Phoebe.' The look

in his eyes was mingled sincerity and hurt. 'Surely you know that?'

His gaze told her the truth, even more than his words. He attempted a smile, but it was more wry than humorous. 'I'm sorry Felicity inveigled her way in here, and that I let her stay to wreak further havoc. If anyone else turns up claiming to have some mega business deal in the offing and I'm not around, just throw them out, okay?'

Her hands flexed against his chest. She hadn't meant to do it, but she could feel his heart beating beneath her fingertips. Could smell the warm, fresh scent of him, and feel the touch of his thumbs as they caressed the base of her throat.

'And if I throw out someone really important and you lose a truckload of money?'

'Then I'll do business with someone else. It's only money.' Max made a low, growling sound in the base of his throat and shifted position to draw her even closer. His hands pressed into the small of her back, arching her into him, and he closed his eyes and breathed in deeply and slowly, as though savouring something he wanted and needed a lot.

'I've missed you, Phoebe. You've done something to me. Made me want things I should know better than to want. I wanted to come home and spend time with my sons, and look at your face across the table. God help me, I can't even explain it, but I only wanted you.'

He kissed her then, standing there in the garage, with nothing but the scent of stale engine oil and musty concrete and too much rain for company. Kissed her mouth, and her throat, and the hollow beneath her ear.

Phoebe wrapped her hands around the strong column of his neck and let him. She wanted this. What difference did it make if she might be sorry later? Later wasn't now and, right now, she had Max right where she wanted him. And he had her.

He raised his head a fraction, but his arms held her fast against him. 'I take it the boys are asleep?'

'Yes.' She nodded, not feeling capable of a whole lot else with the burn of Max's gaze doing all sorts of evocative things to her insides.

'Soundly asleep?' he prompted, and all the air seemed to suck out of the atmosphere around them.

'They've had medication,' she whispered. 'For their colds. They'll sleep heavily, I expect.'

He nodded. Decisive Max. He knew what he wanted. 'Then let's get out of this garage. Much as I've enjoyed talking to you here, I can think of more comfortable places to be.'

When he held out his hand to her, she knew this was going to be more than an invitation to hot chocolate and a toasted sandwich in the kitchen. This was going to be hot Max and toasted Phoebe, coming together in a way she had never believed would happen.

Phoebe wouldn't deny either of them. She would take this gift and hold it close. Max seemed to believe she always lived for the moment. This time she would prove him right. She placed her hand in his.

'You've just showered, haven't you?' He led her through the house until they stood in his bedroom, with only the light from a small bedside lamp to illuminate them. He drew her closer, into his arms where she was surrounded by the scent and the texture and the reality of him. 'Your skin smells of roses.'

'A body scrub I particularly like.' She shrugged, a nervous little gesture that probably spoke volumes, but there wasn't a lot she could do about it.

Max drew back to search her face. 'I have to know you want this, Phoebe. That you need it as much as I do.'

'I'm here.' Her words were the simplest of answers, and the most sincere. As she spoke she raised her arms and wound them around his neck. She pressed her face to his collar-bone, drew a deep breath and sighed her pleasure. 'I'm here, Max, and I want you. Tonight. Together. Just the two of us.'

When he touched her hair she trembled. When his hands closed in the thick strands and his fingers pressed against her scalp, a little purring sound escaped her.

She might have been embarrassed, except that it seemed to have set Max on fire.

'I want you too.' He breathed the confession against her mouth. 'I need to make you mine tonight.'

'Will you do everything to me that I'm aching for?' Her words were bold, despite the trembling in her limbs. 'Will you satisfy this void inside me and make me certain that I'll never ache again?'

'Sweet, vulnerable Phoebe.' He swept her close, battered her defences with the sweep of his tongue, the sheer strength of his want of her, and his determination to slake it.

'Not vulnerable.' Her aggression matched his own. She held him, matching every volley, every sensual, territorial sweep, until he too was breathless. Nothing less would do. 'Not me. I'm strong.'

Max didn't answer with words. Instead, he responded to her with long, drugging kisses and languid, heated strokes of his hands across her body. 'You're beautiful. Incredible. Sexy.'

His words lifted her, wrapped around her like a cosy blanket. A joy swept through her that was unlike anything she had known before and she smiled, suddenly teasing. 'And you're…' she toyed with a button on his shirt '…overdressed for the occasion.'

With a delighted grin, he hastened to rectify the situation. Buttons popped. He flung his shirt aside, then closed his eyes and scooped her against him.

'It feels good to hold you, Phoebe.' As if to prove his words, he smoothed his hands over the long line of her back. 'There's truth in this for both of us, and no barriers.'

With hands that weren't quite steady, he drew her down on to the bed. That trembling touch went straight to Phoebe's heart. She couldn't help but respond to him.

Her hands were in his hair. Holding him. Anchoring herself. Caressing as her breaths rose and fell while Max learned her, held her, cherished her. After a long time, he opened his eyes, gazed deep into her soul and lowered his mouth to hers.

Their lips melded in sweet, longing unison. His hands were strong and confident against the bones of her shoulders.

She touched the planes of his chest with something akin to reverence. Ran her hands through the mat of hair there, then laid her head against his breast and smiled at the racing of his heart.

Her lips touched his shoulder and he trembled. She laid out a hand, fingers splayed, and he sighed something that sounded a lot like relief and joined their hands, fingers intertwining.

'I want to be one with you.' His whispered words were a benediction. 'I see who you were and who you are, and I want you.'

She doubted that he saw either of those things, but she was beyond debate right now. 'For this moment,' she clarified, for her own benefit as much as for his. 'You want me for this moment.'

He shook his head. 'I will make love to you, slowly and thoroughly, until you don't know where you end and I begin. Until we're both as lost as each other.'

For a moment, she fought the promise of it. The sheer, heady delight of it. But it was too sweet, too wonderful to resist. She reached up her arms, embraced him. Held his much larger frame with the strength of her small hands, and drew him to herself. 'I want to fly with you.'

They flew, slowly and steadily, to the pinnacle of the world. It was a shattering place, a place that fulfilled and terrified at the same time. At the end, Phoebe had tears in her eyes for the sheer wonder of it. And maybe a little bit for the heartache that was already building, despite her best efforts to keep it at bay.

Did she regret this?

No.

And yes.

A great deal of both answers. A reluctant laugh whispered from her lips. At least her feelings were strong. They just happened to be equally as demanding on both sides of the fence.

She dozed, snuggled in Max's arms with the uncertainty of the future rumbling quietly in the background.

When she woke later in the night, Max was waiting for her. They made love again, but it didn't quench her need for him—any more than the first time had. She would never stop wanting Max. Wanting this. Wanting all those hopeless things that she simply couldn't have.

Time to put on a brave face, say a few smart, sassy words that fit the situation and put an end to this before the glow disintegrates into something you'd rather avoid.

Max spoke before she could. 'You were a virgin.' He smoothed her hair with his hand. She stiffened—she couldn't help it—and he used his hand to gentle the tension from her. 'I wish I'd known.'

'Did it really matter that much? I knew what I was doing.' She looked at him in the moonlight and forced a relaxed smile.

'Your father was wrong, you know.' He stroked a hand over her arm. 'You were worth so much more than he gave you.'

'How did you know?' She drew back so she could search his gaze with her eyes. 'I never would have thought Katherine would tell you. It was our bosom-buddy secret.'

'It wasn't Kath.' Max shrugged. 'I wanted to know, so I chased it up. Found out what had happened.'

'When?' Phoebe asked. 'How long have you known? What did you find out?'

'That he refused to acknowledge you. Didn't want to know about you. Yet you turned that around, somehow.'

'Not *turned around*, exactly.' Her voice was flat, unemotional. A foil for the turmoil starting to roil around inside her.

Phoebe didn't like looking back. She'd found for the most part that it was a really unproductive, depressing pastime. 'My mother tried to bribe money out of him when she got pregnant, and later, after I was born, too.' Did Max really want to hear this? 'That effort failed, and she eventually dumped me in an orphanage. When I was eleven, I decided I'd had enough of that life. I tracked down my father—she'd never made any secret to me about it all—and told him I'd have him DNA tested and sell it to all the papers if he didn't get me out of the orphanage.'

'He should have taken you in.' Max looked genuinely pained on her behalf. 'He owed that to you.'

'He didn't want me, and I didn't want him.' She pushed herself up on one elbow and idly stroked a hand across his face. Just for the comfort of touching him now, while she still could. 'I wanted a top-notch boarding school and my expenses paid for. That's what I demanded of him, not his company. Certainly not his compassion.

'It's obvious to me now that my threats wouldn't have scared him any more than my mother's did. Maybe he thought I had guts—I'm not sure—but he agreed to pay, provided I left it at that and stayed away from him. That was good enough for me.'

'He was still wrong.' Max's arms clenched hard about her. 'If he knew what he had missed out on, he would be more sorry than he could possibly imagine. I've only lost four years of Jake and Josh's lives, and I feel as though I was robbed of for ever.'

'Do you really mean that, Max?' She had never thought

she would hear Max admit to anything like this. 'What about your decision to keep in the background in their lives? I thought you didn't care much about them.'

'I suppose you thought I never cared about Katherine, either.' His response had a bitter tinge.

'No. I never thought that.' It was true. She had seen from the start that Max loved his sister and wanted what was best for her. Phoebe's issue had been with exactly *what* Max thought was best.

'Let's leave it, okay.' Max pulled her head down until it rested against his chest. 'Let's just enjoy this moment.'

'As if it were the *only* moment?' Although she hadn't moved, she had already started to withdraw emotionally. It was past time, and heaven knew how painful this was all going to be when his arms were no longer around her—when they were no longer close, in any sense of the word. 'I don't fit into your world very well, do I?'

He tensed. 'Do we have to do this now, Phoebe?'

'There's nothing *to do*.' She pinned on a smile, and drew away, out of his arms, back into her own space. 'I'm me, you're you. Never the two shall be in the same room without coming at least to verbal blows.'

'It's not like that. I like the way you are.' His words rang hollow, though.

'Do you, Max? Even with my wild clothing and my moppy haircut and my determination to say what I think every time and to heck with the consequences?' His silence was telling. Phoebe felt herself crumble inside and wondered if she would ever feel okay again. 'We had this much.' From somewhere, she pulled together enough reserves to make her tone calm, almost unruffled, if you didn't count the tense edging. 'It was more than I ever expected and, no matter what, I don't regret that it happened. I think you were the person who had to be first for me.' Pride goaded her to try to salvage something of the situation. 'Maybe now that I've had that, I'll be able to move on.'

Max spoke quickly. 'There's the boys, and your friendship with Katherine. What happened here can't be allowed to interfere, to change things. I think we should talk about this. Sort ourselves out so we know where we're going.'

She gave a sad, funny laugh. 'We're not going anywhere, Max. We've been, and now it's over.'

If he didn't know that yet, she certainly did. They were still as compatible as a horseshoe on a chook's foot. As Vegemite and ice cream, or a bush fire in the middle of a lake. She climbed out of the bed, scooped up her things and headed for the door. 'I'm just the nanny, that's all. Goodnight, Max. Thank you for making me see things about myself that I'd been hiding from. It was time.'

CHAPTER ELEVEN

'THE boys need new clothes. They're outgrowing everything they own.'

Phoebe's announcement came from the doorway of Max's study. He hit the send button on the e-mail in front of him and turned to face her.

Blue jeans. Blue shirt. Tan brogues on her feet, and matching blue socks. Even her hair was plainly groomed. Not an extra set of boggling eyes to be seen.

'Are you quite well?' he asked. 'You haven't seemed like yourself these last few days.'

She was edgy, unsettled. Max recognised the symptoms—he was suffering from the same. But she had made it clear she didn't want to talk, and he wasn't sure where that left him, since she didn't want to get back in his bed either. At least she hadn't said she wanted to leave again. While she was still here, there was hope that he would be able to talk her back to where he wanted her.

Phoebe had become a burning in his blood. He thought about her, wanted her, needed her, all the time. But she had closed herself off from him in every way but one. When it came to encouraging him to develop his relationship with his sons, Phoebe seemed to have taken on a new lease of determination.

'I'm fine.' Phoebe's chin ratcheted upward a couple of slots. 'Couldn't be better.'

'Okay, good.' He didn't believe her, but there would be no arguing with her about it, he could see that. 'I'm glad to hear it. You say the boys need clothes?'

'Yes. I thought that maybe tomorrow I could take them—'

'What exactly do they need?'

'Raincoats, new shoes, jeans, undies.' Phoebe frowned. 'They need to be completely kitted out, really. Does that make a difference? I thought you could just advance me some money and I'd take them into the city tomorrow and take care of it.'

'That's a good idea,' Max said. 'We'll go early. Get their clothes first, then go down the coast a bit, give them some time at the sea. We can spend a night at an apartment resort and travel back the next day. Take it in easy stages so they don't get overtired.'

He had an agenda in suggesting all of this. Of course he did. But he didn't expect Phoebe to argue when this also meant he would be spending some serious time with his sons. She wanted to see that, after all.

'I thought you were going to go back to work.' The words burst out of her accusingly. Her stance was cautious. 'I can take them shopping. I really want this time with them—'

It sounded too much like backing out for Max's comfort. Too much like *I want this time with them before I leave.* He rose from his chair and came to stand beside her near the door. 'It'll do us all good to have a change of scene, don't you think? Unless you don't feel you can *manage* a trip to the coast?'

It was a gamble, but she picked up on it straight away. 'I can meet any challenge my work dishes out. We can all go shopping and to the coast. I'm sure the boys will love the beach.'

Max suppressed a smile, well pleased with his efforts.

A number of long, trying hours into the next morning, that pleasure had faded virtually into oblivion.

'From now on,' he muttered from between clenched teeth as he dragged Jake out from beneath a rack of men's shirts in one of Sydney's major department stores, 'we do this kind of stuff online. To hell with whether things fit properly or not.'

A stifled snort from behind told him that Phoebe had heard him. She had her arms full of boys' clothing. Somehow she had kept her grip, whilst simultaneously stopping Josh from running away from her. On Max's calculations, she and Josh had gone through this routine eight times in the last four and a half minutes.

'Are we about finished here?' Max growled.

The smile she gave him was a work of art in angelic I-told-you-so-ness. 'Yep. We only need to go upstairs to the shoe department and choose new sneakers, boots and sandals, and we'll be all done.'

'Thank God.' Max held Jake by the back of his belt loops in mid-air while his son paddled his legs in an endeavour to escape his grip. 'Let's get moving, then. The sooner we're out of here, the better.'

The boys cried about getting new shoes. They started shrieking the minute they saw the rows of the shiny things and didn't stop until Phoebe had hurriedly got a salesman over to measure them up and told him to mail what they wanted.

Max made sure enough cash changed hands to ensure this plan would be carried out, and they humbly rushed from the shop, tails between legs, red-faced boys in tow. Max seemed to remember he'd had a good reason for pushing his way into this trip but, so far, all he wanted to do was turn around and go back home again.

The beach was better. Max found a secluded spot and they let the boys loose. After splashing through rock pools and running up and down the beach for about thirty minutes, his sweet-natured, well-adjusted sons were back, in place of the monsters from the shopping expedition. Max took a breath and let himself hope things would stay better.

After that, they took the boys into Little Shoal Harbour to

play in a park, then fed them fresh shrimp and curly fries, and ice creams in little tubs.

There was a movie playing in a really run-down movie theatre. The story revolved around an animated bug on a journey of self-discovery and healing. The boys giggled right through it and Phoebe cried when the bug finally got all the kinks out of its sad, demented life.

She cried, and cried, and cried. Max had to lend her his hanky. The one Jake had already used as a face cloth.

'You're sick. You know that, don't you?' Max took her arm as they walked towards the car. Her eyes were still a bit red and puffy and he sighed and pointed to his boys, who were moving along slowly for a change, their attention fixed on getting the last few lollies out of the bag from the cinema's sweet shop. 'You didn't see them crying, did you?'

'It was a very moving story, Max.' Phoebe pulled her arm from his grip and stalked ahead to the car. 'I'm sure I can't help it if your sensibilities have been frozen since the dawn of time.'

Max wasn't sure whether he should laugh or be offended. Instead of doing either, he made short work of the trip to their holiday apartment. Once there, he carried everything in while Phoebe put the boys in the bath.

By the time Max had finished toting things, and had a bit of a look around the apartment, the boys were tucked up in bed, with Phoebe reading *Hiram's Red Shirt* to them again.

'Hiram's my favourite,' Jake murmured, his lashes fluttering as he laid back on his bed.

'Mine, too.' Josh rolled on to his side, flung one arm over his head and fell asleep.

Max watched Phoebe touch his sons, smooth the hair from their brows and linger over them, and wondered if she knew how good she was at this. 'You'd make a good mother.'

The words had been unconscious.

Phoebe paled as though he had plunged a knife into her heart.

He stepped forward, his arms rising towards her. 'What is it?'

'Nothing.' She turned, shaking herself from whatever place she had been. 'Man, but I'm hungry. I hope you're going to tell me you've ordered something up for us.'

He had, and he thought he had himself under control enough so that when the meal arrived he suggested they eat it on the terrace overlooking the bay. It was a high-rise apartment, with a view of sparkling sea stretching into oblivion. A light breeze lifted Phoebe's hair, tossing it gently as they ate the tortellini and smoked salmon salad.

Max pushed a leafy green around his plate and wanted Phoebe. Ate another morsel of salmon and wanted Phoebe. Did she have any idea how much? Did he *want* her to know?

'You were right to do this for the boys, Max.' She raised her wineglass and sipped the pale gold liquid. 'I'm sorry I tried to put you off the idea.'

He smiled a little, but what he really wanted was her lips pursed just so beneath his own. His gaze burned across the distance that separated them. 'Do you really think it was a good idea? They didn't appear to enjoy shopping very much.'

'They're male, active, and four years old.' She speared a piece of tortellini and savoured it slowly. 'Naturally they weren't going to enjoy clothes shopping.'

'Unless we let them demolish every clothing stand in the store.' He could smile about it now, with a glass of wine giving his system a gentle buzz and his boys tucked quietly in their beds for the night.

'They loved the beach.' She leaned forward earnestly, back on her hobby horse. 'You're doing your best to give them happy times, and it's working.'

Instead of recoiling, Max threw it back at her. 'Tell me about *your* childhood. The bits before Katherine met you.'

'We discussed it the other night.' She lowered her gaze and pushed her plate aside.

Max copied the action, waiting until she eventually looked up at him again. 'There are still rather a lot of gaps. It'd be nice if you were to fill them in.'

He stood, scooped up their plates and the remaining wine and carried them inside, then rejoined her. 'I've always wanted to know. You were Katherine's best friend.'

'But not yours.' Her face settled into deep, serious lines. 'We didn't exactly hit it off back then.'

'No.' He leaned his arms on the table. 'But this is now, not then.'

'Yes.' She gazed into the distance, her eyes narrowed in contemplation. 'I'll tell you about my background. I don't see that it can hurt, because that's all it is these days. Background.'

Max didn't quite agree with that. Backgrounds contributed significantly to who and what people became. They might make a person determined to be different, or so complacent or comfortable that they stayed the same. Either way, they had their impact. 'Tell me.'

'Okay.' Phoebe blew out a breath that hinted she wasn't quite as relaxed as she made out. 'Did you know that pole dancing is considered an appropriate and healthy form of exercise for women these days—the ones who can afford the exclusive classes, anyway? If they want to get a bit raunchy, they dress so they can remove an outer shirt during their routine. Women line up to pay to feel erotic in expensive salons where privacy and confidentiality are assured. Fascinating, isn't it?'

'I hadn't heard of pole dancing as a form of upmarket exercise, no.' In the courtyard below them a trio of musicians were tuning their instruments while half a dozen people swam in the sparkling pool. An impromptu concert was about to start happening, by the look of it.

He turned back to look at his companion, and wondered if she had ever pole danced. Somehow, despite the many ways in which she was free and uninhibited, he doubted it. 'What's the significance, Phoebe?'

'My mother pole danced for money, in one sleazy place after another.' She nodded, her eyes blank of expression. 'I was young, but I remember some of the places. The men there. What it used to be like.

'She danced while I hid under a table at the back, and if one of them liked her and she felt like it, she took him home with us. It wasn't upmarket. It wasn't trendy and, frankly, I didn't like it.'

'Ah, Phoebe.' He had *known*. Had known it would have to be something like this, but hearing her say it, picturing that scared little girl hiding on a dirty floor, worrying, wondering if she would be forgotten, left behind, made Max's gut knot.

'My father was one of those men that she took home. She always said later that he was fascinated by her. The idea was, she was going to catch him. Snare him. A wealthy man to keep her in the manner she wanted to become accustomed to.'

'Are you sure? Maybe they cared about each other—'

'You don't need to comfort me, Max.' She laughed, and there really was no bitterness in it—just sadness and acceptance. 'She used to go on about it all the time. About how she got pregnant, hoping he would marry her and, instead, he walked away. When she tried to force the issue, he made it plain he would never take responsibility. She would never be able to make it stick.'

'And she handed you over to an orphanage.'

'After a while, yes. My birth name was Tinsel Townsend; did you know that? I was to be the next generation of exotic dancer, apparently.'

'You're Phoebe.' He reached across the table and took her hand whether she wanted to let him or not. 'Nobody but Phoebe.'

'That's right.' She nodded. 'I held on to that, to the fact that I could be whatever I chose. That I didn't have to be tainted with any particular brush, be it my mother's or whatever else.

'The caregivers at the orphanage were good ladies. They substituted "Phoebe" for "Tinsel" the day I arrived and they realised how much I *didn't* want to be my mother's daughter. I stayed "Phoebe Townsend" until I told them I had a new last name in mind as well. I wanted to be completely different to that other girl—to the one who got deserted.'

Max nodded. 'How'd you get your name changed?'

She shrugged. 'It was unofficial until I contacted my father. He managed the rest for me—I'm not sure how—but it was part of our bargain. I wasn't going to live with my birth name, and he was going to help me to get away from it, and away from everything else that reminded me of it.'

'Did you have friends? In the orphanage?'

She nodded. He didn't think she realised she was squeezing his hand. 'The ladies were my friends. They were the only ones I'd had up to that point, and the only ones I cared about having. I was sorry when I left them, and a bit scared too, but it had to be done.'

'You're the bravest woman I know.' He stood and tugged Phoebe up beside him. 'You've brave and you're smart and you're good.'

Music had started up some time while they had been talking. With one portion of his awareness, Max realised the group were quite good, playing with a mellow bohemian touch that seemed just right for the coastal holiday surroundings. But he had more important things on his mind right now—like holding Phoebe. 'Dance with me.'

'Whuh?' She stared up at him in confusion.

He clasped her hands, raised them, placed them around his neck. 'Dance with me, here and now. The kind of dancing that's right for Phoebe Gilbert, self-made woman. Extraordinary woman.'

'No pole dancing then, I guess.' She gave a crooked smile.

'No. No pole dancing, unless you want to make me your mainstay for the purpose.' Because now that he had her in his arms, he didn't intend to let her go until they had danced this, whatever *this* was, out of their systems, or to its fruition, or whatever.

They did a slow shuffle around the balcony. It was the kind of dance that could be anything you wanted, and Max wanted to hold her, turn with her, dip and sway in unison, two parts of a whole.

She matched his steps perfectly, as though she could read his mind, his body signals. His grip tightened. 'You're good at this.'

'It's in the genes,' she quipped.

He smiled, but the humour faded quickly, replaced by deeper feelings—feelings of rightness at having her in his clasp as the sea breeze wafted over them and the music floated gently up from below. Those reactions bothered him, but not enough to make him let her go. Not yet.

'It's the two of us, enjoying ourselves,' he corrected. 'Enjoying each other.' He pressed his mouth to the crown of her head. Not a kiss, just a contact.

Phoebe sighed, relaxed, and snuggled closer. Her gauzy dress was ideal for the coastal conditions. He gave thanks for whatever it was that had prompted her to wear it as he crushed her closer, the filmy fabric sliding around their legs as they moved.

At the tightening of his hold, she tilted her face up, a question in her eyes. He answered it by drawing her closer still.

'You're a sensual woman, Phoebe, and that has nothing to do with genes or anything else.' He nuzzled the side of her neck and pressed his mouth there before meeting her gaze again. 'That's pure you. Don't be ashamed of it.'

'Max, I'm not sure I think—'

'Then let me be sure for both of us.' He covered her mouth with the briefest of touches from his own. 'Don't think. Just be here, now, with me.'

'But—'

'Close your eyes. Feel us, together, doing something beautiful.'

Max's words filled Phoebe with evocative images. All the more affecting because they were grounded in the reality of their lovemaking experiences. Phoebe stifled a groan as she remembered and, so help her, she couldn't resist.

Couldn't do other than press closer, allow their bodies to move as one. She knew this was wrong. Hadn't she realised it after last time, when she had been alone in her room and all the agony and futility had come crashing down on her? But she was powerless to stop herself, it seemed.

When Max lowered his hands to cup her hips, holding her steady as they swayed in place, her pulse skittered. The heat of his hands through the silky smoothness of her dress produced tingles in every part of her body.

With lips softened by desire, she pressed a kiss to the hollow of his throat where a pulse beat out a sharp tattoo in contrast with their languid movements.

Had she meant it as an invitation? She couldn't have said, but Max groaned and hauled her in. His mouth fused on to hers, plying her with his need. He plundered, stroking her tongue in long, heated sweeps that left her breathless.

She gave the kiss back to him, parried each stroke of his tongue with a foray of her own. The muscles of his chest contracted as she stroked her fingers across the smoothness of his shirt. When she pressed her hands to his hard stomach, he groaned aloud. 'I hope you know you're killing me.'

A sense of power, heady and strong, washed through her. In that moment, she felt she could do anything. *Be* anything she wanted to be. Of its own volition, her knee bent and she wrapped one slender leg firmly around his calf, and slid upward until the muscles in his thigh jumped beneath her possession.

Max gave a strangled moan. 'If this is torture,' he suggested through gritted teeth, 'then I'm happy to suffer.'

He allowed one hand to slowly trail upward from its hold on her hip, gliding over her waist, then up the centre of her body, over her breastbone until he cupped her shoulder in his palm. 'Your body is a miracle. You're so round and smooth and soft.'

She took a deep breath, connected with his gaze and held it. 'I promised myself I wouldn't do this again.'

'Do what?'

'Make love.'

'We're not, at the moment.'

Oh, the man was buying into the semantics of it now, was he? Sticking to the letter of the law? 'Trust me Max, where this is headed, we soon will be, and I thought we had ended it the other night.'

He cupped her breast gently in his hand. 'Would it be so terrible if we hadn't?'

The sensation of his hand there was exquisite. She held her breath, searching for control and finding only shattered resistance.

When she remained silent, he pressed against her. 'I'm burning, Phoebe. I want you so much; I don't understand myself any more. I'm not sure I understand anything.'

'You lust after me.' That was natural. He was a man, she was a woman. They had made love. Because of that, their bodies knew each other. Were bound to want each other again, given the right circumstances.

What could be more appealing than a balcony above a beach in the evening light, with soft music drifting up from below? 'If the whole world went about slaking their lust at every turn, there would be pandemonium. Any person can desire another person.'

'This is more than that.' He seemed confused, as though he was grappling to understand things himself but couldn't find what he was looking for. 'I can't describe the way I feel when we're like this, but it's nothing I've ever had before. You trusted me with your history tonight.'

'What has that to do with anything?' Max didn't *want her*. Not as an equal, anyway. He might want to protect her from harm. Might—God forbid—feel sorry for her.

'I won't lean on you, Max.' If that was what he wanted from her, he was hoping for the one thing she would never give. 'Not ever.'

She wasn't sure whether Max released her from his hold or if she broke away herself, but they were separated now. It saddened her, even though she had pushed to make it happen.

Max moved to the balcony rail and gripped it with both hands, staring out into the distant sea. 'I think this is about more than sex, Phoebe. It's deeper than that. Things are *changing* between us. Don't tell me you deny that?'

'No, I don't deny it.' How could she, when it had tortured her from the moment she had given herself to him? When it continued to torture her, and confuse her, and leave her wondering what the future could possibly hold for her, aside from a breaking away from this man who had been part of her life all these years. This man who had first antagonised her and eventually attracted her.

A sense of desperation engulfed her. It seemed imperative that she convince him that she wasn't as deeply held by all of this as she was. 'I thought you understood—we had to make love that once, to exorcise whatever it was that had built up between us. To be able to get past it.'

Yet the thought of moving forward without ever holding Max that way again, of being close to him that way again, filled her with not joy, but agony. She didn't know what to do about that, except try to hide it from him.

'You want to run. You're refusing to accept that there's something here that matters, and so you're trying to run.' Max's tone held exasperation and hurt. 'It's not the answer, Phoebe. Not this time.'

Her temper exploded. She threw her hands up in the air. 'Then what is? What *is* the answer?' It wasn't as if he wanted to spend the rest of his life with her. It wasn't as if he could *accept* her, *love* her. *Care* for her as a fellow human being worth those responses.

'I don't know what the answer is, Phoebe.' Max's fists clenched and unclenched at his sides. 'You gave yourself to me. You were a virgin and you gave yourself to *me alone*. Surely that signifies something?'

'Maybe any man would have done.' It was a stupid thing to say. Even the thought of allowing another man such intimacy left her cold, but she had her pride and right now she was standing on it. 'It was a glitch in my system, but it's fixed now.'

He ran both hands through his hair and swung to face her. 'Damn it, Phoebe. You said at the time that it meant something to you that it was me.'

'Yes, and I said once I'd got past that barrier I could move on.' What did he want her to say? That she wondered if she would ever have a relationship with another man for the rest of her life, and all because of what she had shared with *him*? 'I'm going inside, Max.' She needed to get away from him, before he realised how close to the edge she really was. 'Goodnight.'

The next thing on Phoebe's agenda was crystal clear to her. She had to ensure that Max and his sons were as bonded as they needed to be, and then she had to leave.

CHAPTER TWELVE

'AND I just don't know what to think, what to do.' The words came out in a wail that might have been embarrassing if Brent hadn't immediately reached over, wrapped a youthful arm around Phoebe and squeezed.

'That's a real bummer.' The young gardener squeezed again then let her go. 'What'll you do? Will you stay on here?'

'I'll have to leave, but I've got to make sure the boys will be all right without me first.' She didn't have the emotional energy left to try to explain how she felt about Max's sons. 'There are issues—things that I want to make sure are sorted out before I go.'

It wouldn't have been right to say anything more. Besides, she had already spilled her guts quite enough for one afternoon.

They were seated on the steps outside Brent's garage apartment. Max had actually gone into the city, although he had grumbled about it. He seemed to have lost his interest in getting back into super work mode for the moment, but this deal was one he had personally committed to some months ago.

Meanwhile here at Mountain Gem, while the boys were playing in the sandpit, Phoebe had found herself pouring out a carefully edited version of her relationship woes to Brent. She had admitted she loved Max, and found that saying it out loud hadn't made her feel a whole lot better.

She sniffed and drew back, and offered a wobbly smile. 'I appreciate you listening to me, and I'm sure I'll get myself sorted out. It was a big help just to have someone else to talk to about it.'

Brent gave her an awkward pat and pulled back. 'Any time. I've got three younger sisters who'll end up going through all this stuff at some stage. With my dad gone, and me the eldest, I figure I can do with the practice.'

He was a nice kid—thoughtful, uncomplicated. A pity he wasn't a few years older. Maybe Phoebe could have fallen for him then, instead of Max. *As if she would have fallen for anyone else on the whole planet but Max.*

'Thanks. I'd better get going.' She hauled herself to her feet, brushed the back of her jeans shorts with her hand, and started down the steps. 'I'll catch you later, I guess.'

She took a couple of good sniffling breaths as she headed for the sandpit, intent on setting herself enough to rights that the boys wouldn't know that she had been crying. 'Okay, guys. Time to go inside and grab a little snackaroo.'

There was no response. She looked up and saw that the sandpit was deserted. With a shrug she tramped inside, figuring they must have just run in, but the house was quiet too.

A niggle of worry descended. The boys had been right there in the sandpit when Phoebe had started talking to Brent. She didn't think she had been with him for more than a couple of minutes, but where were the boys?

'Jake? Josh? Where are you? It's time for something to eat.'

She searched the house and grounds, and then the surrounding outbuildings. By the time she had finished she was starting to panic and Brent had joined her, calling with her for the boys to come out of hiding.

Phoebe grabbed his arm. 'How long was I with you, talking?'

'Five minutes, maybe?' His mouth pursed. 'You don't think they're lost or something, do you?'

'Of course they're lost.' She drew a deep breath and willed herself to calm down. 'Sorry. I'm a bit worried. Do you remember the last time you saw them?'

'In the sandpit, when you and I started talking.' He

shrugged. 'After that, I got absorbed. I wasn't taking much notice of what they might have been doing.'

Brent didn't *need* to take notice, because it was *Phoebe's* job to watch them. Max had left her in charge of his sons, and she had lost them.

They could be anywhere. Could have wandered on to the road, been taken by some passing psycho. Could be subject at this moment to any number of hazards here on the farm or worse.

For a short time, sheer panic overwhelmed her. She froze to the spot and couldn't seem to think. It only lasted a moment before she snapped back to reality and the sick feeling in her stomach. 'They have to be somewhere nearby but if I can't find them quickly I'll have to let Max know what's happened, and organise a more comprehensive search.'

At that moment, Max's four-wheel drive barrelled up the lane and swirled to a stop in front of them.

When he climbed out, he took one look at her face and said, 'What's wrong?'

'The boys are missing. They're not in the house or anywhere nearby.'

Max's face paled. 'How long since you saw them?'

'About ten minutes. I was going to look a little further afield, then if I didn't find them quickly try to contact you and organise a fully manned search.'

His face was frozen into harsh lines. He shook his head. 'I should have been watching. I should never have left you alone with them.'

His words hurt, but her carelessness had proved he had every right to condemn her. 'I'm sorry, Max. I know this is my fault.'

Max turned to Brent and told him which parts of the property he wanted him to search. 'If we don't find them in the next fifteen minutes, I'm calling the police.'

He hurried off in the direction of the nearby apple orchards and fenced-in creek, calling for his sons. Every bit of his focus was tuned to what he was doing. Phoebe could see that, and he probably didn't want her anywhere near him, but she needed to find the boys just as much as he did. She went along with him.

After a couple of minutes of looking and calling, Phoebe noticed a plastic toy dropped on the ground near the fence in the distance. It was almost buried in the long grass. She hurried to take a closer look, then called to Max. 'This toy is from the sandpit. That's the last place I saw them.'

Max called again, more insistently. Again there was no answer, yet the toy meant the boys had definitely been this way.

They climbed the fence and hurried to the banks of the creek and there were Jake and Josh, sitting still as statues, their faces chalk-white.

Phoebe almost fell to her knees, her relief was so strong, but the relief was short-lived. There was something wrong here. 'Wait, Max—'

But he had already bolted forward, calling their names. *His* relief was so clear that it blotted out everything else.

'No, Daddy!' Jake's panicked cry froze Max.

'Max, there's a snake.' Phoebe's voice shook as she pointed beyond Jake to where Josh was practically eyeball to eyeball with the reptile. There were tear tracks on Josh's face and his little body shook. Phoebe didn't know how much longer the boy would hold out, and the snake didn't look too happy either. It's tongue was flicking in and out in a menacing way.

'It's all right.' Max's tone was remarkably even and assuring, given that he looked as though he had lost ten years off his life. 'You're both very brave, and I'm going to take care of this.'

Without taking his eyes off the scene, he lifted a large rock, then stepped steadily forward, warning the boys to stay still. Phoebe stood watching, praying they would do as he said, that they wouldn't panic and try to run.

In moments it was over. The snake's head was smashed beneath the rock. Jake and Josh were snatched into Max's arms, wailing their heads off.

'Did the snake bite either of you?' Max put them down and ran his hands over them. Without compunction, he tugged their clothes out of the way to check them from head to foot.

'No, Daddy.' Josh hitched his shorts back into place with an indignant huff. 'We stayed still, like Phoebe said. *Snake 101* says *Stay. Still. Wait. For. Help.*'

'You was too long.' Jake burst into noisy tears again, and Max again pulled both boys up and into his arms. 'We was there for ever.'

Phoebe choked back her own sobs, turned, and hurried ahead of them back towards the house. The boys didn't need her now. They were exactly where they needed to be. *With their father, who knew how to be responsible.*

Whatever Max's issues had been, they were buried now. There would be no retreating from his sons again. Phoebe was free to go.

Given what she had allowed to happen, it was imperative that she *did* go. Some watchdog she had made in the end. Maybe it was just as well she would never have a child of her own. She clearly wasn't fit to be given such a responsibility anyway.

Once inside, she prepared food and a bath for the boys. Then, while Max took care of them, she went into her room and packed. She waited there with the door closed until Max had the boys settled in their beds for the night.

Then, taking a breath for courage, she picked up her belongings and went in search of Max. He sat in the kitchen in the half dark at the table, the scattered remains of the boys' messy dinner all around him. He still looked shaken, but not as badly as before.

Phoebe wished she could say that she felt any better. She left her bags in the hallway and went to face him. 'I accept full responsibility for what happened. Your sons could have died today, if not from snake bite then by drowning, and either thing would have been my fault. You were right not to trust me from the start.'

'Phoebe.' He went to rise.

She waved a hand, a funny shooing motion that ended with her hand pressed over her mouth while she tried to regain control of herself. 'I deserve every bit of censure you can hand out. By my selfish actions, I put your sons in danger. You love them, Max. I know that you'll protect them, no matter what. That you'll watch over them and give them everything they need, in every way they need it. Whatever was holding you back, it's gone now.'

'It is. I will, but I don't want to talk about that right now.' This time he did rise and came to stand in front of her. 'It was a frightening ordeal for them. For all of us. I spoke harshly to you when I first arrived.'

A broken laugh burst out of her. 'You had every right.'

'I find it hard to trust people, I admit that.' Max ran a hand through his hair in a weary, frustrated gesture. 'But I did trust you. I still do, despite the way I acted earlier. It was just tension. Do you understand? I should have been taking more of an interest in them. If I'd been there too, maybe it wouldn't have happened. It would have lengthened the odds against it, anyway.'

'You shouldn't trust me.' The words emerged in harsh, self-directed disgust. 'I've proved today that I'm not worthy of it. You're being very kind, Max. I appreciate it, but you don't have to pretend. I know what I did, and I know the only answer now is for me to leave. Immediately.'

'What nonsense is this?' He seemed almost angry, as though he had been brought to the end of his endurance by her words.

'You couldn't live with me here now, Max. We both know it.' Her mouth curled into a bitter smile. 'I couldn't bear it, either. Not knowing how I put those innocent little boys into jeopardy with my thoughtlessness. My bags are packed. I only wanted to tell you how sorry I am before I go. I'll get Brent to drive me, so you won't have to worry. Give—give Jake and Josh my love.' She wanted to say more, but if she tried to go further she would lose control completely, and she wanted to leave with at least a shred of dignity still intact.

'I'll do no such thing.' Before she could get past the door, Max's hand clamped around her arm, stilling her. He swung her to face him and bent his head low so there was no possibility of her squirming out of range, or avoiding his words. 'You have to listen to me, Phoebe.'

'But I…' Couldn't he see she needed to just get away?

'But nothing.' He half pulled, half led her back into the kitchen and lowered her into one of the chairs. Then he stood over her, as though he suspected she might try to escape if he didn't keep a careful watch.

Smart man. 'Please, Max.' She hated to beg, but these were desperate circumstances. 'Just let me go before this gets any worse.'

'It isn't going to get worse.' He clasped her upper arms and gave her a gentle shake. 'Because you're going to sit there and listen to what I have to say.'

'All right.' She had no other choice for now, so she would try to conduct herself with dignity, although she wondered if she had the necessary backbone left to get her through. 'I'll listen.'

'What happened to Jake and Josh today, could have happened on anyone's shift.'

'No, it couldn't—'

'Shut up.' The firm command had its desired effect. Phoebe's mouth snapped shut like a trap.

Max nodded. 'That's better. It could have happened at any time, to anyone.' He released her arms, but didn't move away. 'Katherine may not have mentioned it, but I lost her twice when she was a small child and our parents had left her in my care.'

'I didn't know that.' For a moment, Phoebe almost took comfort in the knowledge, but then she shook her head. 'You would have just been a kid yourself then.'

'Well into my teens. Old enough to be trusted.' Max's gaze bored into hers, commanding her continued attention. 'The first time it happened, I scared myself enough that I swore it would never happen again, but it still did.'

Despite herself, she was curious. 'How?'

'I just turned my back.' He shrugged his broad shoulders. 'Frankly, I can't even remember what I was doing when she ran off the second time. All I remember is the utter panic when I realised she was missing again.'

'Did your parents—'

'Go ballistic?' A crooked smile lifted the sensual mouth. 'No. They were well aware of what can happen with little kids. After all, they'd already been through raising me.'

'I don't see what this has to do with me, with my losing your sons.'

'It's just the same.' He touched a hand to her face, just the simplest of caresses, then let it drop. 'The boys got out of your sight and, yes, they could have been seriously harmed, just as Katherine could have been both times I lost her.'

'I don't imagine you had to rescue Katherine from the jaws of a snake.' Phoebe couldn't keep the censure from her tone. It was self-directed and unforgiving, and she planned to keep it that way.

No matter what Max said, she *was* responsible for this. If he thought he could forgive her—and she doubted that was true anyway—she couldn't forgive herself. She never would.

'There was no snake with Katherine, but you did all the right things today, Phoebe. You noticed quickly that they were missing. You started looking immediately. It was also your instruction that probably saved them from being in a far worse state than they were.'

'Oh, how can you possibly say so?' What could have been worse than the sight of those two small children facing the kind of danger they had faced? And all alone because she had lost them?

'I say it because it's true.' His face softened. '*Snakes 101*. You can't tell me it was anyone but you who taught them those rules. I certainly hadn't thought about it, although I should have.'

'They could just as easily have forgotten the rules in the face of danger, Max, or done the right thing and got bitten anyway. It signifies nothing.' Her nerves were frazzling, stretching tighter by the moment until she thought she would snap right in two. 'Please, I can't take this.'

He was silent for a moment, then he nodded. 'All right. We'll leave the matter alone for now. We're both worked up, it's been a rough day.'

Max reached for Phoebe again, cradling her face in his hand. He needed to touch her, and that touch was somehow healing, even though Phoebe was obviously far from being ready to forgive herself.

Reluctantly, he lowered his hand, resisting the urge to pull her into his arms and kiss them both into oblivion. Something told him that wouldn't be the answer right now. 'Go to bed. We can talk about this in the morning.'

She hesitated so long he thought she would never answer, but finally she gave a single sharp nod. 'It would be cowardly not to say a proper goodbye to the boys, so I guess morning *would* be a better time to leave.'

Now it was Max's turn to silently nod, because he had no intention of verbally agreeing to her saying goodbye to his sons. At all.

Max had realised a few things down by the creek today. He needed Phoebe. Needed her to help him while he tried to trust himself with his sons. Needed her encouragement when he worried they wouldn't want him in their lives after all.

And he needed Phoebe herself. Just needed her. He couldn't explain why. He simply did. His first attempt at getting her to commit to him might have failed, but that didn't mean he was ready to give up. Tomorrow, first thing, after he'd had time to think out a battle plan, his campaign would begin again in earnest. 'Goodnight, Phoebe. I'll see you tomorrow.'

CHAPTER THIRTEEN

THE kitchen was redolent with the scents of coffee and pancakes—some of the latter burnt, some not. It was a particularly warm morning, with sunshine streaming unapologetically in through the kitchen windows.

Max stood at the stove in a shaft of that light. His hair was bed-tousled. He had on a pair of khaki shorts and nothing else, and Phoebe's body cried out for the remembered touch of his.

'You're up. Come in.' He waved the spatula from where he stood at the stove. 'We're having pancakes for breakfast, and we're going to need all the help we can get to eat them.'

His words were jocular. The expression in his eyes was set, determined. While she hovered there, his gaze roved over her and returned to her face, and there was heat then as well. He made no effort to hide it.

'Come on, Phoebe.' Josh drummed a syrupy spoon on the table top. 'You's wasting time.'

'Has to eat now,' Jake added with a sticky grin. 'Daddy burnded some, but not all.' He tipped his bowl to a precarious angle. 'See mine?'

'Yes, I see.' Phoebe's gaze went back to Max. She just couldn't seem to help it. As she looked, he gave her that crooked smile. Yesterday, she had told Brent that she loved Max. But today it hit her just how desperately she did.

She glanced at Max through lowered lashes and prayed that he couldn't see her feelings in her eyes.

'Pancake, Phoebe?' Was there a certain inflection in his tone? Did he know?

She squirmed in her seat and kept her gaze lowered. 'No, thanks. I'll just have coffee in a minute.'

Max turned back to the stove.

She greeted his movement with relief and reached for the coffee pot on the table. Her hands were trembling. She had to steady the pot with both of them to manage to pour herself a cup without spilling it all over the place.

Pull yourself together. This is no time to turn into a brainless nitwit.

Then again, hadn't she proved she was exactly that by falling in love with Max? With a superhuman effort of will, she lifted her chin to something resembling the old defiant angle. This just meant it was all the more important that she leave, that was all.

With that thought in mind, she turned towards the boys, rehearsing what she would say to them. Praying she would be able to get through it without breaking down in tears in front of them. 'Jake, Josh—'

'I've been telling the boys how fortunate we all are that you had taught them what to do if they ever saw a snake.' Max spoke calmly over the top of Phoebe's words. Taking up two plates of hot pancakes, he came to the table, placed his down and stepped to Phoebe's side to place the second plate before her. 'We've also had a talk about not going near the creek, and a new impenetrable fence will be going up today.'

'That's good.' She closed her eyes at the torture of his presence so close by that she could smell the blend of scents that were uniquely Max. Could feel his body warmth. 'But really, Max, there's no need to discuss—'

'Eat your pancakes, Phoebe.' Max's hands came to rest briefly on her shoulders and it was such a comforting touch that Phoebe just wanted to turn into it.

She craved his touch as much as she craved his attention and love. *I am so lame.*

He moved away and took his seat but, rather than starting to eat, he cast a steely glance at the boys. 'These two have something to say to their nanny.'

Jake and Josh snapped to attention. Their hazel eyes were solemn, their gazes filled with matching determination. Dear Lord, they were so like Max.

'We's sorry for running off.'

'Yeah. We's very sorry.'

'We won't do it again, ever, 'cause it was bad.'

Josh, caught up in the excitement of the apology, thrummed out a rhythm against his chair legs with his feet. 'We was little brats. Real little—'

'Ah, well…' Max cleared his throat. 'Let's not go into that. You've said your apologies to Phoebe, and it *is* very important that you never do anything like that again. Next time it could be much worse.'

'Thank you for what you've said.' Phoebe reached across the table and clasped the shoulder of first one boy, then the other. 'It's important to me to know that you're going to be safe.'

'It's important to the boys and I,' Max said quietly, 'to know that you're going to be here for them. They want you around. In fact, I've already told them you were worried that you should leave because of what happened yesterday, and they are adamantly opposed to that idea.'

'I can't stay, Max.' As if it wasn't bad enough that she had jeopardised the lives of his sons, she had fallen headlong in love with him as well. She couldn't explain that, so she turned to the boys instead.

'Darlings, you're very happy with your daddy, aren't you?'

The boys nodded.

Phoebe echoed the nod. 'I've been very happy here with you all, but you need a *real* nanny. One who's…' She paused, thinking about what she would want for them if she could have any choice. 'One who's jolly and kind and bakes yummy cakes and things and knows how to go mushroom hunting and isn't afraid of the smell of playdough and dirt and flour glue.'

In her mind's eye, Phoebe pictured someone middle-aged, totally dedicated, kind beyond measure and incredibly responsible.

Someone who wouldn't stuff up.

'But we want *you*.'

'Daddy said you'd stay.'

Both boys appeared to be on the point of either a flat-out rebellion or floods of tears. Phoebe didn't want either and blamed Max squarely for putting her in this position. She glared at him.

He sighed and pushed his untouched food away from him. 'You'd frustrate a saint. Can't you see this is where you need to be?'

'This was only to be a temporary arrangement, Max, right from the start. You wanted someone more mature.'

'And I got someone with an imagination and enough stamina to keep up with them.' He slapped a hand down beside his cooling food. 'Things change. People's wants change.'

Wants, she noted. Not *needs*. 'Yes, and that's exactly the problem.' She cast about for inspiration, and actually found some for a change. 'I want to develop my career path. Move into education rather than only childcare. At least start that degree we discussed.'

'We also discussed a perfectly acceptable way that you could go about achieving that goal, without having to give up your life here.'

Oh, sweet heaven. How could she bear him bringing that up now?

'I can't *M-word* you,' she snapped, glancing significantly at the boys. They might be young, but they weren't stupid. One mention of that idea in front of them, and all hell would break loose. 'I want to m—*you know what*—for love, Max. Not for any other reason.'

She wanted him to refute it. To say that he did love her. That they could build a life together on that basis. He didn't. Instead, he paled beneath his tan. After a moment of silently staring at her, he shook his head.

'All right, Phoebe. If you intend to be stubborn about this, I suppose there's nothing I'll be able to do to change your mind. I'll start interviewing today.'

His face was a harsh mask. 'I trust you'll be able to find it in your heart to give them a day or two? However long it takes me to find someone else? I can't very well watch them all the time and see to that as well. And I *do* need to figure out some kind of work schedule. It'll have to change, obviously, but I can't abandon my business completely.'

'There's daycare.' She grasped at the straw before she remembered this was Sunday. They weren't due to attend the centre until Wednesday.

'Yes, eventually there is.' Max got up from the table, expertly cleaned up his boys without garnering any howls of rage for his efforts, then sent them in to watch cartoons with an admonition not to start kicking anything, including each other.

Then he turned back to Phoebe. 'You will help until then, though?'

It would probably kill her but, with the boys' hopeful faces still etched in her mind and Max looking at her with a mixture of determination and frustration, she capitulated. 'Yes, I'll help until then.'

While Max looked for a new nanny, Phoebe spent her spare moments looking into other possible employment opportunities. Max didn't like it.

He paced his study, restless again, as usual. It was early afternoon on Wednesday. The boys were in daycare. After driving them there, Phoebe had dawdled doing who knew what and had just arrived back with a stack of newspapers, all in duplicate.

'So you can check for nannies at the same time,' she had said, and had sauntered off to her room to look at the Positions Vacant columns.

'You're not scanning the papers.' The accusation came from the corridor outside his study.

He turned at the sound of her voice, and she was already halfway across the room, pointing an accusing finger at the pile of papers. 'They've not even been opened.'

Her accusatory tone, her complete lack of interest in anything other than getting out of his house with as much haste as possible, made something snap inside Max.

'I've looked.' He strode away from her, staring out of the window. 'I've been through dozens and dozens of adverts, I've placed the details of my requirements at no less than ten employment agencies, and I have so far interviewed six candidates for the position.'

'Well, yes, but you haven't employed anyone.' She seemed to recollect herself, grabbed up the papers and brought them over, slapping them against his chest.

Max tossed them on to the floor and swung fully to face her, too angry to mind his P's and Q's. 'Don't push, Phoebe. I really am not in the mood for you to press me about it at the moment.'

'And I'm not in the mood to still be here.' Her words were almost a wail. 'You have to keep looking. Now!'

Max stared down hard into her irritating, desire-inspiring face. 'I warned you,' he said, and he kissed her.

Phoebe's mouth welcomed him, even while her hands rose to push against his chest. He held fast, ignoring those pushing hands, and she kicked out, tried to get clear.

'Don't fight me.' He growled the words at her even as he

asked himself if he was completely insane, and plunged further into the kiss.

She *should* be fighting him. Hell, she shouldn't have to, because he should have put a stop to this before it had even got started. His body, however, had other ideas, and was not at all keen on the idea of giving her up.

'I don't want this,' she gritted.

'Then why are you kissing me back?' The frustration continued to beat at him, all the stronger for the fact that he finally had the reality of her in his arms again. He wanted that. Wanted their lovemaking so much.

Phoebe moaned his name. In resignation? Acceptance? Wanting? Maybe all three. All he knew was that her body sagged, the heat of anger going out of her as they clung together. There was a vulnerability in the gaze that searched his face, as though she were storing a memory while she still could.

'Phoebe. Sweet. Don't deny me this.' He trailed kisses over her face and neck, his body quivering as the hands that had reacted against him now curled into his collar, tugging him closer as she arched into his touch. 'I don't know what's the matter with me.' His muttered words were accompanied by more kisses as he nipped her earlobe, tasted the delicate shell. 'I can't seem to settle to anything lately. All I can think about is you.'

'Really?' She seemed to still in his arms. To hold her breath as her gaze sought his. 'Do you really think about me all the time, Max?'

'Yes.' He ran a hand over the familiar curve of her hip, his body already way ahead of him in remembering what it had been like to make love to her. 'I look at you, and I want you.'

'Sexual gratification.' She drew back slightly. 'That's what you mean, isn't it?'

He wanted her, to a ridiculous degree. So much so that he had offered marriage as part of a package deal to take care of that urge. 'We're good together. There could be a lot more for us, even if you won't consider marriage as part of it.'

The laugh she gave as she pushed away from him had an edge to it.

They stood facing each other for long silent moments before she spoke.

'Don't touch me again, Max.' She stepped further away from him, but her gaze remained steady on his face. 'In fact, I'm going to save you the trouble of worrying about that, and just leave right now. There's no reason why you can't watch the boys yourself until you manage to track down another nanny. Your work will wait, if it has to.'

'You don't have transport of your own. Or a job to go to.'

'Brent can drive me to the train station. I'll ride in to Sydney.' Her shrug was a study of indifference. 'I have friends there I can stay with until I find my feet.'

'What friends? Who are they? Come on, be reasonable.' Given the strength of his frustration with her, he thought his words were quite restrained.

'I don't have to divulge details to you. I'm no longer in your employ and I'm leaving.' She turned away.

Max was about to reach for her, to restrain her and drum into her all the reasons why this move of hers was a mad idea, when the phone shrilled insistently. He swore, stalked past her and snatched it up, barking his name into the receiver.

It was a business call. His operations manager in New Zealand had got himself into a twist over a bidding war and wanted Max to grant permission for the production of two identical pieces so both prospective clients could be satisfied.

Max refused, of course. If he started making that kind of allowance, the Saunders precious gem line would end up selling for a pittance in chain stores. The call took costly minutes. By the time Max slammed the phone back down the house was unpleasantly silent.

A check revealed that Phoebe's things were gone and so

was she, but she had left a terse note on the kitchen table, stating that Brent was driving her to the station and Max had best remember to collect his sons on time from daycare.

The cheek of her. Max slammed aimlessly around the house until it was time to leave, then he stalked outside, climbed into his four-wheel drive, and headed out to get the boys. He'd be damned if he would drive the tin can Phoebe had used, even if he had purchased it. He didn't need the reminder of her, nor the cramped confines.

His mood when he got home was by no means improved. The boys had grumbled when he informed them Phoebe had left and they'd be getting a new nanny very soon to replace her. Then they had played up in the back seat on the way home, niggling at each other and ending up, predictably, in tears when Max had snarled at them.

Now they were sulking in front of the TV. Max had noticed that Brent's vehicle was back. At least he could give his gardener instructions for tomorrow. Brent, at least, might be inclined to listen to him and act like a rational human being while he was at it. Max told the boys to stay put until he got back, and slipped outside to find his gardener.

Brent was in his apartment, the door still open. He had apparently flipped on the TV as he went inside and was watching a news update of a train derailment.

'Let's talk about tomorrow's workload.' Max's tone was on the sharp side. He tried to temper it. 'I've thought of a few things I want you to do on top of your regular jobs.'

'Wait.' Brent put up a hand in a determined *shut up* gesture. 'I'm worried about this.'

Max took a closer look at the TV and, as he did, the news reporter mentioned the train line in question and Brent's concerns became obvious.

They watched the rest of the piece in silence, then Max swung immediately towards the door. 'What time did you put her on?'

Brent told him and Max nodded, trying not to worry too much and failing badly. 'I'm going to call that info number, see what I can find out. I've got the boys in the house, so I'll have to go back.'

'I'll come with you.'

Max nodded and kept walking. When he dialled the information number, there wasn't a lot they could tell him that was of help.

They certainly weren't saying exactly what had happened or whether there had been casualties, and the TV coverage had been shot from overhead and at a distance. But Phoebe had definitely been on that train and that knowledge made Max sick to his insides.

'I'm going to find her.' Max was out of the door before he even registered Brent's words.

'Do you want me to wait here with the boys?' Brent called. 'Or bring them and follow you or something?'

He'd forgotten his own sons. Max swung back, trying to pull his thoughts together. 'I don't know what I'm going to find there.' He raked a hand through his hair. 'I don't want to take them, but I shouldn't leave them. They've never stayed with you—'

'I'll get my aunt Colleen.' Brent was already hurrying to pick up the phone. 'She's only in Penrith, and she's got a car to get herself here. She's very responsible. She and I can watch 'em together. Will that do?'

'Fine, fine.' Max nodded.

Brent cleared things with his aunt and nodded as Max hurried away with a 'thanks' tossed over his shoulder. With the boys immersed in the TV show he hadn't even said goodbye, but he could worry about that later. Right now, all his thoughts were on Phoebe.

Was she safe? He had to find out, and quickly. His gut clenched.

CHAPTER FOURTEEN

THE scene of the derailment was a steep area, running along-side the road. There were ambulances, police and rescue vehicles pulled up. Max parked well back, leaped from the four-wheel drive, and started running.

He had passed two policemen and several other officials, all of whom called to him to stop, before he realised that was *his* hoarse voice yelling Phoebe's name. At the sight of the derailed carriages, his heart lurched into his boots.

'Phoebe!' There seemed to be a lot of people milling around on the embankment, looking dazed. Some were making their way up towards the road. Others were being attended by ambulance crew. Children were crying and people were comforting each other. The driver of the train was being interviewed by police.

Max was only interested in one person. He had to find her, and she had to be all right. She just had to.

'Here, Max. I'm here.'

His gaze swung towards the sound of her voice. He half believed he had imagined it because he so wanted to have heard it, but there she was, rising shakily from where she had been sitting with her back against a tree trunk.

He had her in his arms before he realised what he was doing, and then he hissed out a breath and held her cautiously at arms' length. 'Are you injured? Has someone looked at you? I'll get an ambulance officer over here.'

'I'm all right. Just a few bumps and a bad case of post-adrenalin shakes.' Her smile was wobbly, and a tear trickled down her dirt-streaked face. 'I've been checked, Max. Truly. I was just trying to catch my breath before I worked out what to do next. It's pretty clear this train won't be going anywhere for a while.'

'You're coming home where I can watch over you.' To Max, it was the simplest thing in the world. Anything else would be completely absurd. But first he needed to touch her, hold her, assure himself again that she really was here and safe.

He drew her gently closer and she sighed and let her head rest against his chest. For a long time he simply stood there, cradling her body with his own and thanking God that he hadn't lost her. 'You're with me now. I plan to do everything in my power to keep you safe.'

'There were no fatalities,' she murmured. 'I'm so glad about that.'

'I'd like to know why it bloody well happened,' Max snarled, less inclined to feel cheerful about matters with Phoebe looking as though she'd been hurled off a cliff. It was a steep track—she virtually had been.

'Some idiots abandoned a car on the tracks.' She shuddered. 'How could they do that? We were lucky. The driver saw the obstruction and did his best to avoid a collision. He just couldn't slow the train enough in time. I should still go to Sydney. My friends—'

'If you really did have firm plans, I'll contact them for you,' Max said, 'but you're still coming home with me.' One glance at her face was enough to convince him she hadn't had any plans at all.

'What about my luggage? It was all on the train.'

'If possible, we'll retrieve it later. Until then, you can wear some of Katherine's leftover things. I'll look after you. Don't worry.'

Weak tears tracked down her face and he looked away, knowing she would hate the loss of control. He helped her up the incline and into the four-wheel drive. By then she really was shaking badly. Shock had clearly set in.

Max pulled a thick jumper from the back seat and wrapped it around her shoulders, looked at her white face and, despite the warmth of the day, turned the vehicle's heater on.

When they arrived back at Mountain Gem, she roused briefly, her eyes widening in worry. 'The boys—'

'Are being ably looked after by Brent and his aunt. Wait there.' Max rounded the vehicle, opened her door and lifted her into his arms.

She pressed her face into his chest and let him carry her inside without protest. Even his sons' greetings and questions when they saw them didn't penetrate. Max assured them Phoebe was fine, simply upset and tired, and carried her to his room.

But was she really okay? He second-guessed his decision not to take her to a hospital for an independent assessment, then reminded himself that she had been examined by ambulance officers at the scene and they had declared her well enough. What if she wasn't, though?

'Phoebe? Let's get you out of these things and into bed.' It didn't even occur to him to settle her back into the room she had left just that morning. Phoebe was *his*. He'd had some sort of revelation out there, although he hadn't had time to stop and assess it yet.

He was never letting her go again. That much he knew. Whatever recuperating she had to do would occur in his bed, where he could lie right beside her and supervise it.

He laid her down and brought a warm washcloth from the bathroom to bathe her dusty face and arms. As he cared for her, he noticed a number of bruises rising on her skin and a couple of shallow scrapes. His hands began to shake and he quickly completed his task, then stripped her to her underwear and eased one of his T-shirts over her head.

'Lie down now, love.' He eased her back and tucked the sheet and blanket around her. 'I'm going to get you some tablets to help make you comfortable for the night.'

She nodded, but didn't seem to really be there with him. Max wanted only to scoop her into his arms and hold her and never, ever let go. He stood beside the bed, looking down at her wan face, at the hair tousled into such disarray and the haunted eyes, and his revelation came clear in his mind.

He loved her, and wanted and needed her in his life. She was the only woman he would ever need or want.

Somewhere along the line it had happened, and there was no going back. The magnitude of his feelings almost felled Max.

He backed from the room and made his way to the kitchen. Brent was there with his aunt and Max's sons. They all looked at him expectantly, and Max opened his mouth and hoped that what came out would be coherent. 'She's okay. Bruised and bumped around a bit, but okay.'

'Thank God.' Brent drew a relieved breath, then introduced his aunt.

She was a jolly-looking woman in her fifties and appeared to have made easy friends with Max's sons. Max thanked her for her help and she waved a hand.

'It was a pleasure. To tell you the truth, I've been a bit lonely since my youngest left the nest. I'm a widow, you see, so there's only me now, rattling around the place.'

Max nodded thoughtfully as he reached into the high medicine cabinet to retrieve the paracetamol.

'We thought the boys might like a picnic and sleep over at Brent's flat with us,' Colleen said quietly. 'If that meets with your approval.'

'Thank you.' Max looked into the kind eyes and realised he meant it. 'I'd appreciate the opportunity to take care of her by myself.'

She nodded. 'Yes, lad. I thought you might.'

He kissed his boys and watched while they were shepherded out of the house. Then he went back to Phoebe, to give her the tablets. She was asleep, curled into a ball and not looking particularly at ease or comfortable.

Max wakened her gently and got the tablets down her, then stripped off shoes, socks and shirt and climbed into the bed beside her. When he wrapped her into his arms, she sighed and snuggled close, and that was enough for Max. For now.

Phoebe came awake slowly, and to a number of realisations. Bits and pieces of her ached. She would have bruises, no doubt, but thank God things hadn't been as disastrous as they could have been. She was also warm and pervaded by a sense of safety that could only be ascribed to one source.

A sense of *déjà vu* washed over her. When she opened her eyes, she wasn't surprised to find Max's grey ones looking right at her, concern clear in their depths. His arms were around her, his bare chest pressed to her cotton-covered one.

Glancing down at herself, Phoebe saw she was clad in a T-shirt she recognised as one of Max's, and had no idea how she had got into it. 'Did you put me to bed last night? Did I drag you in here with me? What am I doing in your room?'

'Too many questions, too early in the morning.' His words were stern, but his expression was gentle. 'You'll have to learn to do better.'

Phoebe blinked. 'Well, I—'

Max cut off whatever she might have been about to say—and, truthfully, she wasn't sure it would have made sense anyway—by the expediency of kissing her. Gently. With a featherlight movement of his lips upon hers that made her want a whole lot more.

Phoebe had been through something tough on that train yesterday, and she didn't want to feel deprived at the moment. If Max wanted to kiss her, he could at least do it properly. She snaked an arm around the back of his neck and arched into him, letting her feelings on the subject be known.

Max, fortunately for him, seemed in the mood to comply

with her wishes. He groaned and deepened the kiss, and Phoebe was quite cheerfully wondering if she would ever get to come up for air when he suddenly broke free.

'You're in a fragile state. I shouldn't be forcing myself on you like that. I'm sorry.'

'Oh, monkey bum.' She was about to launch herself at him and *force* another kiss out of him, when her blurred senses cleared enough for her to remember that she wasn't supposed to be doing this at all.

Max didn't love her. The whole thing was hopeless. Instead of going after another kiss, she chewed her lip. '*Did* I drag you in here with me?'

Max eased her down on to the pillows and rested on one elbow above her, watching her. After a moment of this she started to fidget, realising just how much of a wreck she must look, and wishing he wouldn't look quite so kind and sweet and eminently lovable.

'You didn't drag me in here with you,' he finally said.

'Oh, well, that's good then.'

'Did you know that Brent has a lovely aunt named Colleen?' he asked, as he toyed with her hair. 'She's middle-aged. A widow.'

Phoebe tried unsuccessfully to wriggle away from him. 'Um, that's nice, I guess.'

'The last of her children just left home, and she's at a loose end.' He nodded as though pleased with himself. 'I'm going to ask her to take on nanny duties for Jake and Josh. I think she'll agree, too.'

Phoebe hoped her lips weren't trembling. She really didn't feel up to this right now. 'That's good, Max. Really. I'm glad.'

'Yes, so I won't need you here for the boys any more.'

How much cruelty did he intend to heap on? She swallowed over the lump in her throat and nodded. 'I don't imagine you will.'

All of a sudden, Max's expression became deadly serious. 'That means when I ask you to stay, Phoebe, I'll be doing it for me. Not for my boys, not because I feel sorry for you or think I can help you by employing you, either. I've accepted that you're perfectly capable of making your own way through life without any help from me. I want you here for my own sake.'

She didn't get it. Her brows twitched together in suspicion. 'I'm not sure I follow.' Maybe she had taken a knock on the head yesterday that she didn't remember, and it was giving her delusions or something.

'I need you, Phoebe.' He dropped a kiss on her nose, then one on each eyelid, and then he closed his eyes and drew in a deep breath, brushing his lips across her messy hair before his searing gaze met hers again. 'It's that simple because I love you, you see. Quite desperately, as it turns out.'

'You love me.' She repeated it stupidly, just staring at him. 'But you've never said you did.'

'Until yesterday, I didn't know.' He paused, seeming to search for words. 'There's so much I need to say to you, Phoebe. I hardly know where to start. For one thing, I regret the way I treated you when you were younger. I know I handled myself badly at times, trying to control you into doing what I thought was best. I'd never met anyone like you. At every turn you challenged me, and I didn't know how to deal with that. I still don't, but I've realised I can't live without you.'

Phoebe thought back to those childish days. To her antagonism towards Max and her secret longing to have somebody care about her even half as much as Max cared about his sister. The rejection by her mother and father had cut deep. 'I envied Katherine. You loved her so much.'

Max gave a sharp laugh and shook his head. 'I was terrible at parenting her, Phoebe. So bad, in fact, that she begged me to go back to working long hours so she wouldn't have to spend as much time with me.'

'No.' Phoebe couldn't believe Max had thought that all this time.

'Oh, yes.' Before she could refute what he'd said, he went on. 'Why else do you think I was so determined to keep my distance from Jake and Josh? I didn't want them to turn around one day and ask me to back off. I thought it would be better if we just skipped that step. That they'd be happier that way.'

'Oh, Max.' Phoebe had her heartaches. She hadn't realised Max had been carrying this one around.

'They may still push me away some day.' Max's vulnerable words squeezed her heart. 'But they're my sons. I love them. I have to be in their lives, for as long as they'll let me, anyway.'

'Katherine always knew you loved her.' The words burst out of Phoebe.

Max looked at her, his brows raised in mystification.

'She just wanted to be able to spend more time at school. To stay back and enjoy the social whirl. That's why she asked you to go back to working your longer hours.' Phoebe held his gaze with hers, determined that he would hear this and accept it. 'You made her feel secure after your parents died. Secure enough that she wasn't scared to ask for that. She'd be devastated if she realised what you'd been thinking all this time.'

'Then we just won't tell her.' Max laughed. Shook his head. Laughed again. 'Are you sure?'

'I'm sure.' And she was. Absolutely. And it felt good to be able to give him this.

'I want to talk about us now, Phoebe.' He leaned forward and this time when he kissed her it was searing. 'I love you. I want to marry you and spend the rest of my days with you.'

Phoebe realised he meant it. He really did love her. Her

heart soared, then plummeted into the aching hole inside her. 'I can't, Max. You'd regret it. I'm no bargain, believe me.'

'Yes, you are. You're beautiful and talented and wise. The most loving of mothers.' His hands cupped her face gently and his grey eyes, dark with emotion, locked on to her face. 'And I want you in every way there is.'

The moan that passed through her lips was tortured, not rapturous. 'I can't ever be a mother, Max. I can't have babies. I'm barren.'

'What do you mean? How can that be?' His shock was palpable. His arms tightened around her until he was almost crushing the breath out of her.

She eased back and looked into his face. Until now, she hadn't known that a heart could keep on breaking, over and over again. 'I didn't develop like other girls. I've only had two tiny little bleeds in my life. My uterus doesn't work.'

'I wish that wasn't the case.' His voice was tortured.

'It makes everything different.' She nodded, pulling away. Pulling back into herself. 'I know. I understand.'

But Max refused to let her go and stroked his hands gently up and down her back. 'No, Phoebe. I don't think you understand at all.'

He swallowed hard, and when he spoke again his voice was softer, gentler than she had ever heard it. 'I hurt *for* you, that you're never going to get to carry a child and give birth. I wish I could fix that for you, and I hate that I can't.'

'Please, I don't want to talk about it.' His words were just tearing her up inside all the more. Just rubbing in all that she couldn't have.

'But I *do* want to talk about it, Phoebe.' He gave her arms a gentle shake. 'I have to talk about it.' He sat up in the bed and moved until his back rested against the pillows, then pulled her up into the cradle of his arms. 'I'm sorry you can't have a child, Phoebe. I'm sorry with my whole heart. But I'm also glad that you told me, because it's helped me to understand you a bit more. I want you as my wife.' He punctuated the statement with a firm kiss on her mouth. 'And I want you to be a mother to Jake and Josh. You challenged me to let them into my life. Now I'm challenging you to do the same. To accept them, and me. To let *us* be your family.'

She was so overwrought that she couldn't speak at first. Tears leaked from the corners of her eyes and bathed his chest. Hot, achy tears that came from a deep, solitary place inside her that for the first time had a chance of healing. Her barrenness and her empty childhood were all rolled into that one place.

Max stroked the side of her face that he could reach, brushing the tears away with his fingertips. 'And maybe later we could adopt a baby, if that's what you want. I don't care, Phoebe. I really don't. I just want you, by my side, in my life, for the rest of my life.'

He drew her face up until their gazes were locked together. 'I can't live without you. I don't want to. Say you'll marry me.'

'Yes.' She laughed. Cried. Buried her face in his neck and wrapped her arms around him. 'Yes. I want to marry you. To be a mother to Jake and Josh.' A joyous sob choked free. 'To be a family together.'

A deep shudder went through Max and his breath sighed out. 'Thank you. You don't know what this means to me.' He pulled her back down the bed until his body covered hers like a warm, loving, demanding blanket. 'I need you, love you, want you, Phoebe.'

'Do you need me right now?' she wondered aloud as her body clamoured for his.

He kissed her long and deep, then drew back. 'What do you think?'

'I think that's a yes.' Another thought occurred to her and she paused. 'What about the boys?'

'They're in the garage flat, with Brent and his aunt.' He

glanced at the bedside clock. 'It's still very early. I'm sure we won't be seeing them for a while yet.'

Phoebe wrapped her arms around her beloved Max and drew him down to her. 'Then I think you'd better kiss me. For starters.'

And Max obliged.

EPILOGUE

It was the following summer. A warm breeze was blowing, rustling the gum-tree leaves and sighing gently through the apple groves.

They stood at the end of Mountain Gem's long, L-shaped lane. Max, Phoebe, Jake and Josh. And Aunt Hatty.

Back at the farmhouse, Nanny Colleen was probably crying into the boys' leftover cups of breakfast milk. Brent's aunt got a bit emotional on momentous occasions, and the boys going off to elementary school for the first time was definitely momentous. Katherine had been and gone several times in recent months, too, getting to know her nephews, but she wasn't here today.

The bus appeared in the distance, its engine churning as it came along the road towards them.

'Yay, it's here, it's here.'

Jake and Josh started jumping up and down, their excitement palpable.

Phoebe could sense Max's emotion as he stood beside her—as mixed as her own. But she glanced first at Hatty and couldn't help but smile.

Max had turned Australia inside out, searching for what he had referred to as a *real* relative for Phoebe. Someone she could lay claim to from her own family tree. Someone other than her mother and father, that was. Phoebe had claimed she didn't need anyone more, not with Max and the boys to love, but Max had found Hatty. A second cousin once removed on her mother's side, and the most loving of women. Phoebe could only be thankful.

Before Phoebe had known it, Hatty had been installed in

nearby Blackheath. Hatty was a potter by trade, and totally at home in the arty crowd of the town. She took to Phoebe and the rest of the family like a slightly crazed duck to water, and none of them had looked back since.

Happiness swelled inside Phoebe. She did turn to Max then, and smiled into his dear, familiar face. 'You're frowning. They're going to be fine, truly.'

He drew in a sharp breath, nodded and made an effort to relax. 'I know. I know they will. It's just hard to let them go, that's all.'

Max worked three days a week in Sydney these days, and spent the rest of the time at home either working, involving himself in the farm or playing with the boys. It was going to be a wrench for him to lose this amount of time with his sons, but Phoebe smiled. When she wasn't at her part-time uni classes, she would be doing her best to keep him occupied, one way or another.

The bus driver gave a friendly toot of his horn and pulled off the road into the designated loading zone. When the door whooshed open, Phoebe turned and quickly gave each boy a bone-crunching hug. All too soon, they would be too grown up and refuse to let her. She planned to get her licks in while she could.

As Jake and Josh climbed confidently on to the bus and settled into a seat near one of their old daycare friends, Phoebe swallowed the lump in her throat and smiled big and wide for them. This was their day.

'Bye-bye, littlies.' Hatty waved a pink handkerchief as the bus moved off.

Phoebe waved. Max waved.

Hatty started away up the lane, murmuring about challenging Colleen to a game of cards while she didn't have the boys under her feet and blowing her nose nostalgically into that same pink handkerchief.

When the bus disappeared Max pulled Phoebe into his

arms. She buried her face against his chest, but felt she had to give a token protest. 'I don't need comforting, you know. I'm coping with letting them go.'

Max's laugh rumbled against her ear. 'Who said it was *you* who needed the hug?'

Their lips met and clung and Phoebe smiled against his mouth, grateful for this. For all of it. She had Max, the most loving husband. Two beautiful sons who had simply taken her on as their new mother and never looked back.

And now...

'You haven't said much about that last specialist appointment.' Max's words were tentative. As he spoke, he hooked her arm through the crook of his elbow and started back towards the house. He didn't look at her and Phoebe knew he was holding back from interrogating her.

The specialist doctor was one Max had insisted on when she had admitted she had never had her condition looked into. If nothing else, he wanted to ensure that there was nothing happening inside her body that might hurt her either now or later.

It had turned out that there wasn't. In fact, the specialist had felt she had a chance of having a baby one day. Maybe. If circumstances smiled. He'd handled other cases of women who rarely or never had their periods and had still managed to conceive. He had insisted that he wanted to keep seeing Phoebe. To monitor her. And there were still options as yet unexplored.

Phoebe hadn't cared. She really hadn't. She had Max and the boys. Her heart was full, and there wasn't a day that went by that she didn't wake up smiling, thankful. Happy. She kept up the appointments more for Max's sake than her own.

Now, she turned her face to smile at him. 'Actually, he talked to me about *in vitro* fertilization.'

Max's brows went up. He didn't quite manage to hide the sliver of hope that sprang into his eyes.

She smiled, teasing him just a little, because she could. 'Yes. That's what he mentioned, but it's not an option any more.'

'Oh.' Max nodded, smiled for her, even though his face had fallen at first. 'Well, that's okay. It doesn't matter, right? We've talked about it before, and we're cool. We can adopt later, if we want…'

He trailed off. Maybe because Phoebe was smiling fit to crack her face.

She laughed. 'Aren't you going to ask me why I'm grinning?'

'Okay.' He looked at her as though she was mad, but he obliged, as she had known he would. 'Why are you grinning like a loon?'

'Do loons grin?' She tilted her head at an inquiring angle. 'What encyclopaedia did you read that in?'

'Very funny.' He grabbed her and lifted her off the ground. 'Tell me why you're grinning, or I'll keep you up here all day.'

'I'm grinning because IVF is no longer on the agenda.' She slid slowly down until she was back on her feet, then took his hands in hers and held them. 'And IVF—' she touched his palms to her tummy '—is no longer on the agenda because we already took care of it.'

'How?' Max looked at her blankly. 'I don't understand. Are you saying something else has happened, so you know for sure you never can conceive now?'

'Nope. Not saying that. We're pregnant. Twelve weeks.' She rubbed his hands gently, watching his face as the news sank in. 'I've got a bump there and everything. Feel?'

'I just thought—' He broke off. Searched her face with stormy, excited, hopeful grey eyes and shook his head. 'Are you sure? Has he done tests? Are you okay? Is the baby okay?'

'I'm sure.' She smiled. 'He's done tests, I'm okay, the baby's okay.'

A hoarse cry ripped from Max's throat. He lifted her into his arms, twirled her around until she was laughing and dizzy, and then kissed her with his whole heart in it.

When they separated, they both had tears in their eyes.

'Do you want this, Phoebe? I never really asked.' He hesitated. 'I guess I didn't want to go on about it if it might never have happened.'

'I want it.' This time it was she who drew his head down and pressed her mouth to his. 'I want it because I love you, and because we've been given this despite the odds. It's a chance for both of us to have something we thought we'd missed out on. For you, to see the baby from the start. For me, well, the same and more.'

'Yes.' Max's voice was hushed. 'I love you, Phoebe. I love you so much.'

'I love you too.'

And she did. That was what was so special about it.

Desert Heat

Susan Mallery
Alexandra Sellers

On sale 19th August 2005

*Available at most branches of WHSmith, Tesco, ASDA, Martins,
Borders, Eason, Sainsbury's and all good paperback bookshops.*

FREE

4 BOOKS AND A SURPRISE GIFT!

We would like to take this opportunity to thank you for reading this Mills & Boon® book by offering you the chance to take FOUR more specially selected titles from the Tender Romance™ series absolutely FREE! We're also making this offer to introduce you to the benefits of the Reader Service™—

- ★ **FREE home delivery**
- ★ **FREE gifts and competitions**
- ★ **FREE monthly Newsletter**
- ★ **Books available before they're in the shops**
- ★ **Exclusive Reader Service offers**

Accepting these FREE books and gift places you under no obligation to buy; you may cancel at any time, even after receiving your free shipment. Simply complete your details below and return the entire page to the address below. You don't even need a stamp!

YES! Please send me 4 free Tender Romance books and a surprise gift. I understand that unless you hear from me, I will receive 6 superb new titles every month for just £2.75 each, postage and packing free. I am under no obligation to purchase any books and may cancel my subscription at any time. The free books and gift will be mine to keep in any case.

N5ZEE

Ms/Mrs/Miss/Mr......................Initials ....
BLOCK CAPITALS PLEASE

Surname ....

Address ....

....

....Postcode ....

Send this whole page to:

The Reader Service, FREEPOST CN81, Croydon, CR9 3WZ